SIGNED, SEALED...DECEASED

A Cozy Mystery Anthology

BEACHES AND TRAILS PUBLISHING

BEACHES AND TRAILS
PUBLISHING

Contents

Publisher's Note   v

Foreword   vii

DEAD LETTER DAY   1
Daisy Landish

DEATH BY MEMOIR   21
Andrea Barton

IF YOU READ THIS, I HAVE BEEN
MURDERED   41
Gabbi Grey

THE MYSTERY OF THE MISSING
MERCHANT   61
Iris March

THE ROAD TRIP   79
Albert N. Katz

THE TIFFIN-BOX THIEF OF RUE DES
JASMINS   97
Rachel Desiree Felix

THE POSTMAN ALWAYS DELIVERS…
EVENTUALLY   117
Flora McGowan

LAB'S LABOURS LOST   135
Melissa Behrend

THE STORK BROTHERS THING   155
Daniel Fox

STAMPED, SEALED AND DUVAL   175
Denise Landry

A LETTER FROM THE PAST   189
Andrea Tillmanns

BON AMI   203
donalee Moulton

Contributors   221
About the Publisher   225

Publisher's Note

There's something irresistibly mysterious about the mail—the anticipation of an unexpected envelope, the romance of handwritten letters, the knowledge that every delivery carries a story.

For our first anthology, we invited authors to explore postal, delivery, and communication-themed mysteries: stories involving letters, missing packages, messages from the past, or unexpected deliveries—each leading to murder and mayhem. From over thirty submissions, twelve exceptional tales emerged.

We're particularly proud to feature a Canadian guest editor alongside six talented Canadian contributors, with stories spanning from Quebec City's cobblestones to British Columbia's remote islands. International voices from the UK, Germany, South Korea, Australia and the US complete this global collection, proving that mystery travels on every mail route.

You'll meet amateur sleuths who stumble upon decades-old crimes, postal workers turned detectives, and ordinary people forever changed by a single delivery. Whether it's a mislabeled 1944 love letter, a rare stamp worth killing for, or threatening notes revealing family secrets, each story reminds us that the past demands its due—postage paid in full.

Consider this anthology your invitation to a world where every envelope might contain a clue, and every delivery could be someone's last.

Happy reading, and remember to always check your return address.

The Publishing Team

Foreword

If you're a cozy mystery lover, you are in for a delightful treat. And if you're not, you will be after reading these enchanting stories.

What is a cozy mystery, you might ask? A story that whisks you away to a charming locale where scenic oceans or babbling brooks, cobblestone streets, museums, flower shops or bookstores play a pivotal role (you get the picture). A story where relatable characters draw you into their world, a world where a delicious mystery must be solved without graphic scenes or explicit language. A puzzle to be unravelled in a safe, comforting place.

Be prepared to be whisked off to a scenic island off the British Columbia coast, a quaint English village, a plant shop in the US Midwest, charming Montreal and boisterous New Orleans, just to name a few of the settings for enigmas that draw you into their journeys to resolution. You'll love the feisty characters you will meet: retired friends solving a local time capsule mystery, a headstrong yet intelligent student, a loving grandmother to her postal carrier grandson, a crusty PI jaded by romance, a young woman grieving her lost sister, a widow grieving her recently deceased—or murdered, husband. These relatable characters bring their stories to life, inviting you into their communities to disentangle curious conundrums.

Many of our twelve authors have won awards in crime fiction, romance and other genres. Their skills are evident in the fabulous tales they have crafted for this anthology. They made my job as editor joyfully easy, and I thank each one of them for their professionalism and kindness. I am awed by their talent.

Thank you, dear reader, for embarking on these mysteries with us. Pull up a comfy chair, steep your soothing tea, and enjoy *Signed, Sealed...Deceased.*

Lena Samson, Guest Editor

Dead Letter Day

Daisy Landish

THE COEUR D'ALENE post office smelled like dust, ink, and boiled coffee—a scent that reminded Maddie Moreau of her childhood library, though somehow less magical and significantly grumpier. She tapped her mittened fingers on the counter as the clerk rummaged behind the scenes for her missing package. Somewhere among the bins and sorting carts was a sheet of vintage postage stamps—bright, illustrated beauties meant to accompany a book-themed silent auction next weekend. Maddie had sourced them from a private seller in Maine. Supposedly pristine. Definitely irreplaceable.

"Sorry, Miss Moreau," said Mr. Shipley, the clerk with a comb-over as patchy as the carpet. "It got routed through Spokane for some reason. Things get weird when the barcodes smudge."

"I understand," Maddie said, though her tone suggested otherwise.

Shipley turned back toward the shelf and pulled a padded envelope from the wrong bin. "Here. This was flagged for your box too. Might've been what the system logged. Not your name, though... Must've been misfiled."

He handed her a battered manila envelope, creased at the corners, with a fading postmark and an ornate wax seal that had cracked clean through. Across the front, in shaky block letters, someone had written:

'Return to sender. Deceased'

Maddie blinked. "Definitely not mine."

Shipley frowned. "Odd. Must've fallen into your slot when the bin tipped yesterday. We've been short-staffed since Marcie's gallbladder incident."

He sighed, rubbing his forehead. "And my niece Tammy keeps stopping by asking for 'temporary loans.' Said something about a 'business idea' involving true crime podcasts. I told her, I work in postage, not publishing."

"Well, if it's not mine..."

"Go ahead and toss it in the 'out' bin," he said, waving vaguely toward the corner. "We don't process dead letters here. They usually get redirected to Boise, but no one knows what happens after that. Black hole, probably."

Maddie turned the envelope over in her hands. The return address was smeared. The recipient's was local, though—Coeur D'Alene. On Oakridge Lane.

And the stamp. She squinted.

A violet 1940s stamp, perfectly preserved, featured a winged Victory figure and the words *Win the War*. Her brows lifted. It was genuine. Rare. The kind of thing collectors swooned over and dealers tried to counterfeit.

"I'll... make sure it gets handled properly," Maddie said, slipping the envelope into her tote bag next to a box of peppermint tea and a paperback mystery with a Yorkshire terrier on the cover. Shipley had already moved on to the next customer, a retiree mailing soap to grandchildren in Florida.

Outside, snow flurried down in determined spirals. Maddie tugged her hat lower, wrapped her scarf twice, and started the walk back toward Mike's office. Her fingers itched to open the envelope. She was fully aware that tampering with mail could be a federal offence—but wasn't it more of a gray area when the mail was already undeliverable?

Especially if it was about to vanish into a dead letter depot where stories went to die. Maddie was, above all else, a lover of untold stories.

She paused beneath a lamppost, squinting against the snow, and broke the seal. Inside was a single folded letter. Cream paper. Black ink. The elegant loops of wartime cursive.

March 14th, 1944

My darling Rose,

I shouldn't be alive. The wreckage was total. But I woke up in a village with no name and strangers who spoke no English. It's been four months since the plane went down. And all I can think of is you...

Maddie pressed a hand to her chest. Whatever this letter had meant—whoever had written it—it had never reached Rose. But someone had tried to send it again.

And now... someone was very much *dead*.

———

BY THE TIME Maddie reached Mike's office, the snow was falling harder—wet, determined flakes that clung to her coat and sparkled on her lashes like she'd stepped into a snow globe. She stomped her boots on the mat just inside the door and called out, "I brought tea, gossip, and a federal offence!"

Mike Malison looked up from his laptop, his dark-rimmed glasses perched low on his nose. "Please tell me you're not serious about the last one." She dropped the tote onto the desk between them and plucked out the envelope, now carefully flattened between the pages of the terrier paperback.

Mike took one look and raised his brows. "That looks... ancient." He rubbed his temple. "If I'd known going free-lance as a data analyst would involve so many cold cases, I'd have stuck to algorithms."

Maddie grinned. "You love it."

"I love spreadsheets. You love ghosts with postage."

"It is. Dated 1944. I found it at the post office. Wrongly routed to my box." Maddie perched on the edge of her chair, cheeks pink with excitement. "It's a love letter, Mike. From a man named Edward, presumed dead in the war, writing to a woman named Rose in Coeur D'Alene. It never got delivered. But someone *tried* to send it recently."

Mike set the laptop aside. "How do you know it was recent?"

Maddie pulled out the envelope again. "The original wax seal is cracked and someone resealed it with clear tape. The ink on the front, 'Return to sender. Deceased' is in modern ballpoint. And this stamp." She pointed. "It's the real deal. A rare wartime issue. But the way it's placed? Slightly skewed. Likely added by someone trying to pass it off as original."

Mike leaned closer, frowning thoughtfully. "So, someone

found this old letter and tried to make it look like it had just gotten lost in the mail? But why?"

"Exactly the question I asked myself. And why now? Why to a local address?" Maddie opened her laptop and tapped the address into a property records database. "97 Oakridge Lane. Belonged to a Rose B. Whittaker from 1942 to 1985. Died unmarried. Left the house to a distant cousin who sold it."

Mike tilted his head. "So, Rose never got the letter."

"Or she did—later. But here's the twist." Maddie opened a second browser tab. "There's no official death record for an Edward Harrison matching the details in the letter. But there *is* a military report from 1944 stating he died in a plane crash over the Ardennes. No body recovered."

Mike's eyebrows climbed. "So, he might've lived?"

"Or someone *pretended* to be him. Or someone found his letter and used it for some other reason." She sat back, crossing her arms. "Either way, someone went out of their way to put that letter into the system. And now it's here."

Mike stood and crossed to the office kitchenette. "Well, nothing pairs with mystery quite like tea." He started boiling water.

"I'm thinking," Maddie said, fingers tapping the armrest, "we start at the local historical society. See what they've got on Rose Whittaker. If there's any mention of Edward. Diaries, photos, census records."

Mike looked over his shoulder. "You think there's a scandal hiding in a seventy-year-old envelope?"

Maddie grinned. "I think there's a story that was meant to stay buried—and someone just tried to dig it up."

Outside, the snow fell faster. In her coat pocket, the envelope felt heavier than paper had any right to be.

THE NEXT MORNING, the storm had calmed, but the sky hung low and gray like a held breath. Maddie clutched her thermos of lukewarm coffee and pushed through the glass doors of the Coeur D'Alene post office, the same envelope sealed in a clear plastic sleeve inside her tote. She hadn't been able to stop thinking about the letter. Or the stamp. Or the fact that someone had tried to send it again— seventy years late.

Today, she wasn't here to snoop. Officially, anyway.

She wanted to return the letter, document the oddity, and maybe persuade the clerk, Mr. Shipley, to share a little gossip about the lost mail bin. But the lobby was eerily silent. No waiting line. No bell. No cranky muttering about holiday cards arriving late.

"Hello?" Maddie called gently, stepping around the corner toward the back counter.

That's when she saw it.

The door to the sorting room stood ajar. One of the fluorescent lights overhead flickered. And just beyond the counter, half-concealed by an overturned bin of manila envelopes, lay a pair of polished black shoes. Attached to feet. Attached to…

"Oh no," Maddie breathed.

She darted around the counter. Mr. Shipley was slumped on the floor, one hand clutching his chest, the other resting palm-up beside a tipped cup of coffee and an open bin marked 'DLB – Dead Letters.'

His eyes were open but vacant.

And there, not two feet away, was a corner of the WWII envelope—its twin, or maybe its original—peeking out from the pile of dusty, undeliverable mail. Maddie backed up, heart pounding. "Okay. Don't touch anything." She grabbed her phone and hit speed-dial.

Mike answered on the second ring. "Hey, I was just thinking about that stamp—"

"I found Mr. Shipley," Maddie whispered. "He's... he's dead. At the post office. You need to call Carson."

There was a pause. "On it. Don't move."

Maddie ended the call and glanced around the room. A dark glove lay on the ground, caught beneath a crate. A red smear marked the edge—maybe ink, maybe something worse. A bottle of correction fluid sat uncapped on a nearby shelf, and the sorting machine hummed softly, still cycling mail that would never be delivered.

She knelt just close enough to confirm what she already suspected: Shipley was gone. A quiet, solitary man who had once told her he'd worked the same post office for thirty-six years and had *never* lost a package—though he admitted to rerouting a few that 'didn't smell quite right.' Now he'd become a dead letter himself.

Outside, the wind picked up again, rattling the old glass panes in the front door. And somewhere in the mess behind the counter, someone had left a secret they hadn't meant to.

BY NOON, the post office was roped off with yellow tape, a 'CLOSED DUE TO UNFORESEEN CIRCUM-STANCES' sign hastily taped to the door. Maddie stood just outside the barrier with Mike, nursing her second coffee of the day and trying not to shiver. Not from the cold, but from the strange feeling that the letter in her tote bag had cracked open something much bigger than a forgotten love story.

Detective Carson Luttrell emerged from the building looking uncharacteristically grim.

"Shipley had heart issues," he said, nodding to Mike. "But the medical examiner's initial look suggests he didn't die naturally. There's bruising along the jaw and trace chemicals on the cup near his body. We're running tests, but it's looking like poison."

"Poison?" Maddie asked, eyes wide. "From a coffee mug?"

"Possibly. Or absorbed another way." Carson glanced at her. "You said he gave you the letter yesterday?"

She nodded. "By accident. But... I think he knew something about it. He looked surprised when I brought it up. Nervous. And when I came back today, that letter—or one that looks just like it—was lying outside the bin near him."

Carson raised an eyebrow. "You think the letter's connected?"

"I think someone doesn't want it traced." She paused. "Or maybe someone *does*—but only part of it."

Carson scratched his jaw. "The 'dead letter' bin might've gotten a little too lively."

AN HOUR LATER, Maddie and Mike sat in the tiny upstairs reading room at the Coeur D'Alene Historical Society, where Maddie had sweet-talked her way into the private archives. Mrs. Harriet Geller, a retired librarian and expert in 'local romances and minor scandals,' pulled a thin folder from the filing cabinet marked 'Whittaker Family – Oakridge Lane.'

"Here we go," she said, adjusting her spectacles. "Rose Beatrice Whittaker. Born 1920. Never married. Worked as a piano teacher until 1983. Attended church socials but kept to herself. No children. No known siblings. Died of natural causes."

Mike scanned the death certificate. "No mention of Edward."

"That's the thing," Maddie said. "According to the letter, Edward Harrison was her fiancé. Presumed dead in 1944. But there's no engagement noted in her obituary."

Mrs. Geller pursed her lips. "Oh, I remember Rose. Lived next to that quiet man with the birdhouses—Mr. Mercer. She used to bring him rhubarb jam."

Mike looked up. "What do you know about him?"

"Not much. Bit of a recluse. Walked with a cane. Kept to himself even more after Rose passed." She sniffed. "Always smelled like ink and old cigars."

Maddie's eyes lit up. "Ink?"

"Deep red. Ruined my gloves once when he shook my hand at the post office."

Mike and Maddie exchanged a glance.

"Does Mr. Mercer still live there?" Maddie asked.

Mrs. Geller shook her head. "No, no. Moved into Riverbend Retirement last year. But he still visits the house sometimes. Says it helps him think."

"Think about what?" Mike asked.

Mrs. Geller shrugged. "Whatever old men think about, I suppose. Regrets. Rhubarb. War stories."

Maddie sat back in her chair, heart thudding. A man with red ink on his hands. A quiet neighbour of Rose's. A potential secret identity.

She pulled the letter out again and studied the signature at the bottom.

Yours forever,

Edward

"Mike," she said, voice low. "What if Mr. Mercer wasn't just Rose's neighbour... but her missing fiancé?"

BACK IN MADDIE'S sunlit kitchen, the letter lay flat between two bookends, weighted carefully at each corner. Maddie hovered over it with tweezers in hand, a magnifying glass perched on her nose. Mike, seated at the table with a bowl of kettle corn, watched her with mild concern. "You know, this is starting to look like surgery."

"I found a seam," she murmured. "A second fold tucked under the first. Whoever resealed this envelope was careful, but not *that* careful."

Mike leaned forward. "You think there's another letter inside?"

"Or a continuation. Something they didn't want noticed right away."

She eased the inner flap free.

A second page emerged—thinner, more fragile, yellowed by time. Unlike the first, this one wasn't written in sweeping, romantic cursive. The handwriting was small. Tight. Uneven.

To whomever finds this:

If Rose never saw my words, that was my doing. I mailed the first letter—but I came home, too. I took another name, another life. I watched her from a distance for years. She looked for me in every parade, every church pew. And I—coward that I was—stayed away.

Maddie's hand stilled.

I feared what she'd say. What I'd become. I lived as Thomas Mercer. I buried Edward Harrison when I stepped off that train in Spokane with no papers and no courage. But I never stopped loving her.

She exhaled. "Oh."

Mike stood, reading over her shoulder. "So, Mercer is Edward. He survived the war… and hid in plain sight?"

"He lived next door to the woman who thought he was dead. Who mourned him. Who brought him jam."

Mike pointed to the bottom of the letter. "There's more."

I placed this letter in the post box the day Rose died. I couldn't carry it anymore. I thought maybe it would disappear with the rest. But I never expected it to come back to me. If someone is reading this now… I'm sorry. I never meant to hurt anyone. I only wanted to be forgotten.

Maddie let the page fall flat. Silence hummed around them, broken only by the soft clink of the radiator.

"So, it *was* sent," she said. "He mailed it after her death. He wanted closure—his own way."

Mike rubbed the back of his neck. "But someone found it. And brought it back into circulation. And now a man is dead."

Maddie's eyes narrowed. "And if Mercer wanted to be forgotten… why was the letter in Shipley's hands *again*? Why now?"

Mike's expression shifted. "Unless someone used it. Someone who found it in the dead letter bin and thought it could be… leverage."

"Blackmail?" Maddie said.

Mike nodded. "If someone knew Mercer's secret—that he wasn't who he said he was—it could have been worth something. Or someone might've wanted to expose him just to stir things up."

Maddie grabbed her coat. "Then I think it's time we paid Mr. Mercer a visit."

Mike held the door open for her, eyes serious now. "Let's hope we're not too late."

RIVERBEND RETIREMENT HOME smelled like lemon polish and distant television. Maddie clutched her tote against her side as she and Mike stepped into the sunroom, where a group of residents played dominoes under a crocheted 'WELCOME, SPRING!' banner despite the snow outside.

"Thomas Mercer usually keeps to himself," said the aide who greeted them. "He feeds the birds. Doesn't like loud noises. You'll find him near the end of the east wing. Room 114."

Maddie thanked her and led the way, her boots muffled on the thick beige carpet. Mike walked beside her, quiet.

"Do we tell him about Shipley right away?" he asked.

"No. Not until we know what he knows," Maddie replied. "Let's see how much guilt he's carrying first."

They knocked gently. The door creaked open.

Mr. Mercer sat in a worn recliner by the window, a flannel blanket draped across his lap. A wooden cane leaned nearby. He looked up, gray eyes sharp despite the haze of age.

"Visitors?" he asked, voice gravel soft.

Maddie offered a warm smile. "Hello, Mr. Mercer. I'm Madeleine Moreau. This is Mike Malison. We're not police, just... curious citizens. We have some questions about an old letter."

For a flicker of a moment, his expression didn't change.

Then: "She got it, then. After all these years."

Maddie's breath caught. "Rose?"

He nodded. "I mailed it the day after her funeral. Thought maybe—just maybe—the universe would do what I never could."

"And yet," Mike said, stepping forward, "it ended up in the dead letter bin. Then somehow back in your hands. Then in ours. And now Mr. Shipley is dead."

Mercer stiffened. "Dead?"

"He was found yesterday in the post office," Maddie said gently. "Not a heart attack. Poison."

Mercer closed his eyes. "I didn't... I wouldn't..."

"Did he know who you were?" Mike asked.

A pause.

Mercer swallowed. "A month ago, he came by here. Said he found something strange in the old logbooks. Asked if I was... Edward Harrison. I said no. Of course, I said no."

"But he kept asking," Maddie said.

"He came again. Said maybe the historical society would be interested. Or the papers. Said it was a 'patriotic deception turned personal scandal.' Wanted money to keep quiet."

Maddie and Mike exchanged a look.

"That's blackmail," Mike said.

"I gave him a cheque. Told him it was all I had."

Mercer's voice cracked. "I was so careful for so long. I kept that letter hidden for decades. I thought I could bury Edward with Rose. But I shouldn't have mailed it."

Maddie knelt beside him. "Did you ever threaten him?"

"No. I begged him to stop. I think... I think he enjoyed the leverage."

"And the envelope?" she asked. "The one you mailed?"

"I dropped it in the box near Oakridge. Same one Rose always used. Then I came here. That was a year ago."

Mike crossed his arms. "Then who took it from the bin and tried to resurface it now?"

Mercer's gaze shifted toward the corner bookshelf. "I don't know. But someone was watching. Someone who wanted me exposed—or punished."

Maddie stood. "And that someone may have silenced Shipley permanently."

Maddie hesitated at the door, then turned back. "Mr. Mercer... do you think Rose would've forgiven you?"

He didn't answer at first. Just looked down at his hands, folded tight in his lap like pages pressed shut.

"She forgave me the moment I stepped off that train," he said quietly. "I just didn't have the courage to let her say it."

Maddie nodded, her throat tight. "She waited for you her whole life. I think, in her heart... she never stopped."

They thanked Mercer and left him staring out the window at the flurries beginning to swirl again. As the door clicked shut, Mike turned to Maddie.

"I don't think he did it."

"No," Maddie agreed. "But someone who *knew* he was Edward—and wanted revenge—might have."

Mike's jaw tightened. "Time to find out who else had access to the dead letter bin."

AT THE COEUR D'ALENE post office, Detective Carson met them at the back entrance, ushering them past the still-shuttered front. The crime scene tape had come down, but tension lingered like dust.

"We went through surveillance footage from the last two weeks," Carson said as he led them through the sorting floor. "Most of the rear cameras were down due to maintenance. Surprise, surprise. But one angle caught someone entering the restricted area late Sunday."

He handed Maddie a printout. Grainy, but clear enough.

"Susie?" Maddie asked, recognizing the dark ponytail and signature red puffer jacket of the part-time clerk.

"She had the night shift," Carson confirmed. "Claims she was sorting returned parcels. But what was she doing handling dead letters?"

Mike looked over her shoulder. "She served Rose Whittaker too, back when she was still active. She must've known her from back then. They knew each other."

Carson's eyes narrowed. "Now she works here part-time and was the last person seen near the dead letter bin before Shipley died. You're thinking personal motive?"

"She wouldn't have cared about Edward Harrison," Maddie said. "But maybe she cared about *Rose*."

THEY FOUND Susie seated in the staff break room, sipping tea from a chipped mug. When Carson entered, she straightened—caught between defiant and afraid.

"We need to talk about Mr. Shipley," Carson said, taking a seat across from her. "And about the letter."

Susie's jaw tensed. "I didn't kill him."

"No one said you did," Maddie said gently. "But you knew about the letter, didn't you?"

Susie's hands tightened around the mug. "Rose was my godmother. She never married. She never stopped waiting for him. I used to help her sort mail when I was little—she'd tell me stories about Edward. Her ghost stories, she called them. Said he'd died a hero."

Mike sat beside her. "And then you found the truth."

"She gave me a letter Edward never mailed. Not the original, but a copy—something she said she found among his things after he passed. She told me to burn it if she ever died, said it was a piece of her past that didn't belong to anyone else. But I couldn't bring myself to do it. I told myself I was protecting her memory—but maybe I just wasn't ready to let go."

She looked down at her mug. "When I got the part-time job at the post office last spring, it felt like a sign. I didn't have full access, just the front counter and the return shelves...but I knew the layout, the routines. I'd watched Shipley work those bins for years."

"One night, after closing, I slipped the letter into the dead letter pile. Figured it would vanish. Get lost in the void. Like she always joked dead letters did."

Carson raised an eyebrow. "But it didn't?"

"No. A week later, I panicked. Started imagining someone opening it, reading her words. Judging her.

Judging Edward. So I pulled it out when no one was looking. Tucked it behind a stack of undeliverables, thinking that would be the end of it."

Her hands trembled around the mug. "No," she whispered. "Shipley found it. He thought it was a historical curiosity. Started digging. Found Mercer. When he figured it out, he got greedy. Said he'd 'monetize the drama.' Wanted to sell the story. Said it would 'play well with a war hero's fall from grace.' "

"So you decided to stop him," Maddie said.

Susie shook her head violently. "I confronted him. Told him it wasn't his story to tell. That Rose deserved better. I… I didn't think he'd really go public. But I swear I didn't poison him."

Carson's expression softened. "We'll need to verify your timeline. But the forensic team found red ink on the glove near his body—same brand you use for sorting return-to-sender letters."

Susie's face crumpled. "I only grabbed the bin. I swear. I didn't touch his coffee. I didn't even *see* the envelope until he waved it at me like bait."

Maddie leaned in. "Then who else had access?"

A long pause. Then: "His niece, Tammy. She came by last week. Wanted money. Again."

Mike's eyes widened. "Did she know about the letter?"

Susie nodded. "Overheard us arguing. I didn't think anything of it… until he turned up dead."

THREE DAYS LATER, Coeur D'Alene had returned to its usual rhythm: snowbanks at the curb, paperboys on bikes, and neighbours waving over hedges. Inside the Quiet Grounds Café, Maddie stirred honey into her tea while Mike scrolled headlines on his phone.

"Tammy Shipley confessed this morning," he said. "She laced her uncle's coffee with digitalis—claimed it was just to 'make him sick,' scare him into cutting her a cheque. Said she didn't know his heart condition was that bad."

"She didn't want him selling the story either," Maddie murmured.

"Because she wanted to sell it herself," Mike said. "Only she hadn't counted on someone else already being emotionally attached to the truth."

Maddie exhaled, letting the steam from her cup warm her cheeks. "Poor Susie. All she wanted was to protect Rose's memory. And Mercer—Edward—he just wanted to be forgotten."

Mike leaned back. "Kind of ironic, isn't it? All those years, he was terrified of someone digging up the past. And in the end, the past came looking for him."

"I think Rose would have forgiven him," Maddie said softly. "She spent her whole life waiting for a ghost. Maybe it's better she never knew the full truth. It would've hurt."

Mike reached over and gave her hand a gentle squeeze. "You did the right thing, donating the letter to the historical society."

Maddie smiled. "With the second page sealed. Let people remember the romance, not the regret."

They sipped their drinks in silence for a moment.

"Promise me something," Mike said at last.

"Hmm?"

"If you ever get an envelope marked 'Return to Sender – Deceased,' just… bring it to me first. Or a priest."

Maddie laughed, the kind of laugh that crinkled her eyes and made the barista look over with a grin. "Deal. But only if you promise not to write any letters you don't plan to send."

"Noted," he said. "Signed. Sealed. And very much alive."

Outside, the sun broke through the clouds, setting the snow-topped trees sparkling like silver. And somewhere across town, in a quiet retirement room lined with bird feeders and books, an old man sat by the window—no longer hiding, no longer running. Just watching the sky.

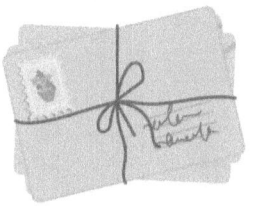

Death by Memoir

Andrea Barton

WHEN I ADVERTISED my inaugural Mansfield Writers Retreat, I never imagined it would end in tragedy.

Five days. Five authors. Led by journalist Jade Riley. Escape the city and work with an intimate group of writers at the gateway to the Victorian high country, Australia.

I borrow my parents' house for the week, ten minutes out of town, a 1980s gem with cathedral ceilings, exposed brick walls and many bedrooms. High on a hill, bathed in the scent of eucalypts, it boasts idyllic views over Lake Eildon. Autumn leaves splash orange and purple, while a shimmer of green sneaks up through the sun-scorched grass.

For four days, the authors craft their projects in a wide spectrum of genres: romance, fantasy, historical fiction, poetry, and memoir. My favourite part of the week is my one-on-one sessions with each of them.

On the last day, I'm in my bedroom before breakfast, finishing my feedback on the authors' final writing exercise, when a scream echoes from the south wing bathroom.

Everyone comes running to find Agnes, the historical fiction novelist, her dimpled face frozen in shock, pointing at the tiled floor.

Harry, the memoirist, lies there, pale and still as the porcelain bathtub. He's folded in on himself—human origami. Nothing like the sturdy man he was yesterday.

We huddle in the doorway, stunned into silence. I pull myself together and check for a pulse. Nothing but cold skin.

Harry's wife, Scarlett, the romance novelist, drops to her knees, her floral dress caressing the floor, and shakes him. "Harry, Harry, wake up!" Head bowed, she kisses his cheek. Loose curls fall from her upswept hair. Red lipstick stains his face. She looks up, then frowns at two empty insulin vials on the vanity unit. "Why would he use that much?"

Nobody replies.

"Why? Why has he done this to me?" Scarlett moans.

She seems to assume suicide—unless she's deliberately misleading us—but I don't. Harry showed remarkable commitment to publishing his memoir. I can't believe he'd check out before seeing it through. The hairs on the back of my neck prickle. If he didn't kill himself, who did it? I've seen no signs of a break-in, and in our remote location, we'd have seen or heard an intruder, which means one of the four authors in front of me orchestrated a fatal over-dose. I shudder.

In crisis management mode, I usher everyone out of the room. "I'll call an ambulance."

Before I follow them, I scan the room to see how his final minutes played out. No signs of a struggle. I take phone photos of the body, the vanity, and the vials, and leave.

HARRY'S SUSPECTED insulin overdose is an unnatural death, so the paramedics call the police, and Sergeant Ali Papatonis, an old pal of mine, asks us to leave while his officers swarm the house collecting evidence.

Late afternoon, we return and stand at the door, watching an ambulance kick up dust as it winds down the long driveway, taking away one of our own. Scarlett runs after it, startling a flock of sulphur-crested cockatoos into the brooding sky. Every bit the heroine from one of her novels, her beauty seems ageless, although she's over fifty, perhaps five years younger than Harry. I bet she wishes she declined my invitation to the retreat, which I extended when interviewing her about her latest novel. By far the best-known author in our midst, after she posted her acceptance on social media, the remaining tickets sold in hours.

The poet, Randall, of similar vintage to Harry, rushes to comfort her. When I first read his poem, 'Skewered Love,' I couldn't decide whether to classify him as a genius or a complete tosser. After five days together, I see him as a brilliant, troubled soul. His gloomy diatribes about politics and constant references to self-annihilation would put any counsellor worth their degree on edge… and even an armchair psychologist would notice the chemistry between him and Scarlett, who'd known each other long before this retreat.

Their writing shares a theme of impossible love— tortured souls wracked by guilt, unrequited love and broken hearts. Yesterday, they disappeared for a toilet break at the same time and returned with flushed lips, crumpled clothing and his black turtleneck sweater untucked from his blue jeans. Clearly, they'd been getting expressive with more than their manuscripts.

Harry must have known about their affair. Maybe that's why he was writing his vindictive memoir, which he introduced as follows:

> Harry Davidson began his career as a property developer but abandoned the big dollars for his true calling in literature. In this tell-all memoir, he lifts the lid on his marriage to Australia's top romance novelist, Scarlett Davidson, and confesses his darkest truths.

The chapter I read describes falling in love with Scarlett in all its racy detail. Despite an excessive use of clichés, his writing impresses me more than Scarlett's new material. She must have a remarkable editor.

The two other authors hang back on the doorstep. Agnes and Bailey, nearly two decades younger, remain outside the tawdry love triangle, both in ostensibly stable relationships. At thirty-one, I'm the youngest of the group.

Out of habit, or perhaps intuition, I check my phone, reassured by the familiarity of its scuffed cover. An unread email from Harry makes my heart take off faster than a startled kangaroo. A message from beyond the grave? When I return to my senses— obviously, a ghost would find a more occult method to impart its message—I see Harry sent it last night; I've just been too busy to notice.

Dear Jade,

I know editing isn't really your game, but after our discussion today, I believe you're the right person to help me refine my manuscript. I've attached my 80,000-word memoir, Behind the Romance. Please send me a quote with timing for when you can you fit this in.

I haven't told Scarlett that I've approached you, so please keep this in strict confidence.

Regards,

Harry

It takes all my self-restraint not to rush to my bedroom to binge read it right away. This confirms my suspicion of murder… why would he ask me to edit his memoir if he didn't hope to see it in print? Further, if Harry dished the dirt on his wife's liaison with Randall or some other scandalous secret, his memoir might hold a powerful motive to kill him before he published it.

But how did the culprit do it? Harry had a stocky build, with bulging biceps and tree-trunk thighs. None of us could have overpowered him. And if someone had tried, we'd have heard the commotion in the morning quiet. Had someone tricked him or tampered with the vials?

Bailey, the fantasy novelist, reaches a hand to my arm, his robe-like jacket wafting sandalwood aftershave. "You okay? You look pale." His goth aesthetic—long brown hair, mascara, maroon nail polish—matches his edgy tales set in the world of vampires, necromancers and rat-men chasing a magical McGuffin.

My mind whirls. If I share my suspicion, I'll put the murderer on guard. And if the memoir motive is correct, I might put myself in danger. But by saying nothing, I'll leave the three innocents unaware of the criminal in their midst. I opt for self-preservation. "I'm fine. Just shocked."

"Me too." Agnes does look peaky, not that I blame her

after discovering Harry's body this morning. She strikes me as someone who feels life deeply.

As a circuit breaker, I say, "Let's go inside for coffee."

"Or something stronger. Should we ask them?" Bailey gestures to Scarlett and Randall, who stand a fairy's breadth apart, heads bowed.

"I'll do that. You and Agnes go ahead." I jump on the opportunity to observe the lovers and slip in a few questions. According to homicide trends, the intimate partner should always be suspect number one. Without Harry, Scarlett is free to pursue her relationship with Randall. She can also control what happens to Harry's memoir. I itch to read it even as I stroll to her, attuned to signs of guilt.

She looks up as my feet crunch on gravel. Rivulets of mascara run down her cheeks.

I gesture to the house. "Let's have a drink."

Randall places a guiding hand on the small of Scarlett's back, and we head inside. My second suspect: the lover. His motives mirror Scarlett's—to pursue their relationship and to prevent exposure. The answers may lie at my fingertips.

We reach the kitchen, where Agnes and Bailey are clearing debris from our abandoned breakfast. I'm not aware of any connection between them and Harry, but I can't help wondering whether they aren't here by chance but by design; Scarlett told the world that she and Harry would be here.

Come to think of it, earlier this week, Agnes had cornered Harry and held a heated debate about property development. I had to call time out before she turned my writing retreat into a fight club. With a PhD on Charles Dickens and the Industrial Revolution, she's well-placed to write historical fiction involving revenge for coal mine deaths. Her startling green eyes shine with intelligence and an uncanny knowing.

Unable to withstand the allure of Harry's memoir any longer, I excuse myself and sneak into my bedroom. I take out my laptop and open the document in Harry's email. Before reading it, I save a backup copy to an online folder. Faced with the file, I consider how to sift through 80,000 words to find incriminating evidence in the time it takes to go to the bathroom. In desperation, I commit a grave sin and turn to the final chapter:

> A writer reveals himself in words, and I hope by now I've shown myself to be a creative soul, if also a foolish one. I'm the first to admit I could have handled my marriage better. The trouble was our relationship and careers were inextricably linked—we fell in love writing a novel together. High on love and success, even though I'd penned most of it, I encouraged Scarlett to take all the credit. It made sense. She loved the limelight and lapped up author visits to book clubs, interviews and book signings.
>
> All the while, I was writing the next one. And the next. We couldn't conceive children, so we birthed book babies instead. I poured all the love and care I would have given a child into our creations.

In a flurry of keyboard strokes, Harry had destroyed Scarlett's credibility. I stared out the window across the sweeping blue-green hills to the mountains on the hazy horizon. What did Harry have to gain by speaking out? And why now?

You may wonder why I'm revealing this now. Has the lustre worn off our love life? Or is it retribution for my wife taking greater pleasure in the arms of Randall Wilson than in mine?

Yes, Randall, I know all about your assignations with my wife. All those lies Scarlett told about going to the gym... I guess she was getting a workout of sorts. Don't bother accusing me of libel because I have evidence. I took up photography to avoid the indignity of hiring a private investigator. A long-range lens can see right through your window from across the street. You should have pulled the curtains.

If death by memoir exists, this is a masterclass. Harry was antagonising those who had wronged him, drawing out his enemies.

I'm not after revenge. And I'm not after fame and glory. Like I said, Scarlett's the one who loves being in front of a camera. Under the spotlight, I hem and haw and get heart palpitations. I'd rather be anywhere else.

What I want—

A rap at the door. "Jade, are you okay?" It's Agnes.
Darn it. "I'll be right there."
I'm about to snap my laptop shut when I pause... if I tell the others I have Harry's memoir, the murderer might give themselves away in trying to delete it. Rationalising that Harry's death overrules his request for secrecy, I leave my most precious possession in full view of the bedroom door, lid open. My computer holds my story ideas, my manuscripts, my innermost thoughts; allowing someone else

to put their hands on it is like letting someone plug an electrode into my brain. But it's a worthy sacrifice. I turn on my GoPro camera and hide it under a blanket, aiming the lens at my computer.

Back in the kitchen, the sombre group sits around the old oak table, without any of the vibrant conversation we shared over the last four nights. They've opened a white wine blend from a local winery that has a lemon and peach aroma. Bailey offers me a glass, and I hesitate before accepting it, recalling his obsession with potent arcane energy.

Agnes pours herself another glass. "What now? Can we leave?"

I check my watch. The retreat officially ends in two hours. "If you're up for it—" I incline my head at Scarlett "—let's gather in about an hour to debrief and say goodbye."

Scarlett agrees, perhaps relieved to be told what to do. Grief does strange things to a person. So does guilt.

I take a gamble and lay my trap. "It's probably too soon to think about this, but will you publish Harry's memoir? I haven't finished it yet, but if it delivers more punches like the bit I read, it'll be a huge success. A special way to honour him."

Scarlett's malaise lifts. "You're reading it?"

"Yes, he emailed me a copy." I down my wine and shove my phone in my pocket. "I'm going for a quick walk. Anyone want to join me?" They won't come if they want to access my computer, so if they join me, they're pretty much cleared in my eyes… unless… maybe this isn't the smartest idea. What if the murderer targets me instead of the laptop?

Scarlett springs out of her chair. "I'll come. I need some air."

I hide my surprise. The others decline, so I head outside with suspect number one. A premature lick of winter chills the air, and rain threatens. I wish I'd put on a jacket. As we stroll around the house, I maintain a safe space between us, ready for any quick moves. We wind through a hotchpotch of fruit trees, wattles, and gums. A sweet-smelling lavender bush reminds me of my grandma. Beyond the back fence lies native forest, hectares of uncleared land, dark and forbidding to a city slicker like me.

"Harry's memoir..." I keep my voice casual. "How much of it's true?"

Scarlett walks head down, arms crossed against the cold. "What do you mean? He hasn't let me read it."

"Did Harry write your novels?"

A tear trickles down her cheek. "Yes."

"And the affair? Randall?"

"Also true. But Harry didn't care, not really. He's had so many lovers over the years that fidelity ceased to matter." She wipes her nose with the back of her hand. "Can I trust you with a secret?"

"Of course." My story antenna switches to high alert.

Scarlett draws a long breath. "The memoir is a publicity stunt. Book sales have dropped, and Harry thought a controversy would help. But it's pointless now. I won't be able to write anything new without Harry. My career's over." She chokes back a sob.

I'm not sure I believe her. Something nags at the back of my brain. "I haven't read all the memoir yet—I skipped to the final chapter, hoping for a summary, but I'm only halfway through. Do you want to finish reading the chapter with me? There might be more."

"Good idea."

I pull out my phone and open Harry's memoir from the cloud. Scarlett huddles close, reading over my shoulder. I scroll to the point where I'd left off.

What I want, dear readers, is a child. Flesh and blood. Not book babies. And not the person who claims to be the child Scarlett gave up for adoption. You can imagine my shock when I intercepted a call from Scarlett's progeny after years of grappling with the disappointment of my wife's infertility.

When I confronted Scarlett, she admitted she could conceive, she just didn't want children. All this time, she'd misled me. I'd stuck by her, shared the loss and invested all my energy into creating a different kind of legacy. Call me selfish, but I refused to pass on her child's contact details. It didn't seem fair for Scarlett to have the privilege of parenthood after depriving me.

This tome is my offspring. All mine. Nothing to do with Scarlett.

Only it's all about Scarlett, isn't it? I'm strangled by the wicked grip of irony—

Scarlett's face crumples.

"I didn't know he was writing about my baby. We had a huge row about it some years back, but I thought he'd come to terms with it."

My mind makes associations at a million miles per hour. If Harry had prevented the lost child from meeting Scarlett, he or she had cause to remove him. "Did you make contact with the child?"

"No, Harry never let me. I—"

"Can I ask a personal question? How old are you? It's just… How old would your child be?"

"Thirty-three." Scarlett blinks rapidly. "My son would be thirty-three."

"Isn't Bailey about that age?" I muse.

Scarlett grips my arm. "What if it's him? What if he was looking for me and came here to meet me?"

"We could be wrong." I backtrack, wishing I'd kept my thoughts to myself. "He's around the same age, but—"

"I need to talk to him." She darts away before I can stop her, a dragonfly chasing a mosquito. Obviously, she hasn't made the mental leap that if Bailey is her son, he had reason to kill Harry.

And what about Agnes? Does she, too, have a motive? One evening, she grilled Harry about his early career. He claimed he left his job in property to fulfill his creative urges, but what if he resigned for another reason? What if he made a fatal mistake?

Harry postulated that "a writer reveals himself in words," and Scarlett's manuscripts— which are actually his —feature tortured souls wracked by guilt. Also, in his book blurb: '[he] confesses his darkest truths'. What I've read so far reveals Scarlett's and Randall's affair, but Harry's confession is buried in 80,000 words.

I search the document for 'mistake,' but nothing significant comes up. 'Guilt.' Nothing. 'Regret.' And there it is: Harry's confession.

All this pales into nothing when I consider my greatest regret—the part of my life I pretend never happened. The real reason I turned from property development to writing. We were demolishing a building rife with asbestos. I hired what I believed was a reputable company to deal with it but they took shortcuts, and five workers ended up with mesothelioma.

I was absolved in the ensuing investigation, but I still feel the blight of guilt. Maybe that's why I accepted not having children; I didn't deserve them after depriving others of their loved ones. I chose a career in literature because I couldn't kill anyone else that way.

My heart bleeds for him living with that shame. His words cry out for redemption, but it's too late now. His business killed people, just like the coal mines in Agnes' novel. Coincidence?

I search the internet for a list of people who died in Harry's incident. Maybe I'll find a link to Agnes. Alas, the last names don't match and I see no other obvious link.

The hour is nearly up, so I hustle inside and check my bedroom. My laptop has disappeared. The sight of the charger coiled on the ground like a snake makes my fists clench, but even as righteous fury sweeps through me, I'm gratified to find my theory validated. Someone stole my *de facto* brain, and chances are it's Harry's murderer. I turn to my GoPro for evidence, but it, too, has vanished. The thief was thorough. Today has cost me a lot—my laptop and GoPro—although not as much as Harry.

Now certain he was murdered, I call Sergeant Ali and beg her to return. She's reluctant—they've already written off Harry's death as suicide—but after I explain the potential motives in the manuscript and my stolen laptop, she capitulates.

An enormous sob draws me to the living room, where I find Scarlett facing the window, staring over the inky lake that mirrors the menacing clouds. Bailey gives her shoulder an awkward pat. "I wasn't adopted. I have pictures of Mum holding me in the labour ward after I was born." He steps away, arms dangling by his sides.

She turns to him. "I'm so sorry. I never should have said anything, I just hoped..."

She pulls herself together as the others arrive, and we perch on the edges of the worn leather lounge chairs for our final meeting.

"Does anyone know where my laptop is?" I affect nonchalance but study their reactions, hoping for a tell.

The authors claim ignorance.

Agnes plays with the hem of her teal sweater. "Where did you last use it?"

"My bedroom." I regret bringing it up. Now that the culprit knows I'm looking for it, they might move it. I need to keep everyone within sight until the police arrive and search their rooms. "I'll find it. I must've left it lying around."

I carry on. "Thank you for coming this week. I'm beyond sorry about... everything. Scarlett, if I can do anything to help, please let me know." I offer a strained smile, and her eyes well. "It's been an honour working with each of you. I'm in awe of your talent, creativity and dedication. Bailey, I'm sure your quest will return gold. Agnes, may retribution give your character the resolution you need. Randall, I hope you meet your true love. Scarlett, trust yourself and you'll find your own voice. And Harry...

may you rest in peace." I pause, willing the police to hurry. "As a tribute, perhaps we could all say a word or two about Harry, if that's okay with you, Scarlett?"

An engine drone draws our attention outside, where a police car approaches in a blur of white and blue. Four spines stiffen, and silence falls over us. I let it hang. If I've learnt one thing in my journalist days, it's that silence makes people uncomfortable. Whoever breaks it first is the most antsy.

But dammit, they all speak at once.

"Why are they here?" Scarlett asks.

Randall rolls his eyes. "Not again."

Bailey jumps up. "I'll be right back."

Agnes mutters, "The police are like bloody capeweed. You can't get rid of them," and excuses herself to the restroom.

I want to keep everyone in the room but I can't stop them, so I rush outside and greet the officers.

Sergeant Ali says, "You're nothing but trouble, Jade Riley," but she sets up in the kitchen and tells us to wait in the living room until we're called to give a statement. Scarlett goes first. Twitchy and watchful, I sit with Randall. Bailey returns from whatever mischief he was up to, but Agnes has been gone a suspiciously long time. I stand to check on her just as she comes back.

On a hunch, I say, "All week I've been trying to figure out where I've seen you before. You look like an old friend of mine. What was your maiden name?"

Agnes takes her seat. "I kept my name when I was married, just like you."

Dammit, my theory about her sharing a family name with someone on the list of asbestos-related deaths plummets. Wait! I grab my phone and thumb furiously, testing another hypothesis. What if it's not Agnes who's out for revenge? I search to see whether Randall was ever married, or whether Bailey's mother had a different name.

Randall heads out for a toilet break. I scroll faster. Just as I find information about Randall's dead wife—she, too, kept her maiden name—the back door creaks.

"It's Randall," I say, rushing to the door. "Tell the police."

I charge outside and scan the grounds. There. Movement between the trees. I take off as the storm kicks in. Pelting rain draws an organic scent from the earth. Randall bolts towards the back fence, my laptop tucked under his arm. If he gets away, we'll never find him or my electronic brain again. He pulls up the top strand of barbed wire and clambers through the fence. His sweater snags.

I close the gap between us.

He peels off his pullover and leaves it hanging. Now in a black t-shirt, he sprints on.

I slip through the fence. His sweater protects me from the barbs. The downpour makes the ground treacherous, and I struggle to remain upright as I enter the forest.

Shouts come from behind. Sergeant Ali. If I look back, I'll slip. Cold air bites my lungs. Brambles grab my jeans. I hurdle a wombat hole, and a wet branch slaps my face. Twigs crack.

Randall is taller than me, but he's ungainly. I'm not super fit but I'm nimble. And I'm fuelled by anger. My legs pound, arms pump. I throw myself forward and clutch his shoulders. He staggers under my weight. Our momentum topples him forward, bringing me with him.

We hit the ground. Randall cushions my fall. My

computer lands in the mud. He's face down, winded. I keep him pinned as Sergeant Ali arrives.

She asks me to move and pulls Randall to his feet. "Come with me. I'd like to ask you a few questions."

I scramble for my laptop, check that it's okay, then stand, panting, hands on knees. "Ask how his wife died."

Randall baulks. "You think I killed Harry?"

"Did you?" I ask.

Sweat trickles down his brow. "No. I swear. Yes, my wife died of mesothelioma. I wanted payback but I didn't kill him. I stalked Harry and stole Scarlett as retribution. I came to the retreat to rub our affair in his face."

And all this time, I thought it was for the privilege of my mentoring. "So why'd you run with my computer?"

"I didn't want my relationship with Scarlett to come out."

"Okay that's enough." Sergeant Ali nods towards the house. "Come with me."

She heads away, keeping Randall in her sights.

My breath returns and I follow them, hunched to protect my computer from the rain, mulling over the case. I still don't understand one thing: how did Randall get Harry to take so much insulin?

I'm so absorbed in my thoughts that I miss it at first: a disturbance near the base of the lavender bush. My spine tingles with anticipation as I crouch and scrape the loose soil aside. About fifteen centimetres down, I find a small glass cylinder. A full vial of insulin. I look for Sergeant Ali but she's already inside. I can't touch the evidence, so I photograph it with my phone and compare it to the ones I took earlier at the crime scene. The vials are identical.

Back inside, after washing my hands, I wipe my laptop

clean and hide it in the closet. My mind whirls, eager to nail Randell. Why would he hide a full vial of insulin? Maybe he replaced it with another one he'd filled with poison. Harry would've noticed an extra vial, so Randall had to take one of his and hide it. When Harry unknowingly used the poisoned vial, he died. Randall could then have injected him with another dose of insulin and left two empty vials to make it look like suicide. My theory tracked, but how to prove Randall did it? He'd have used gloves to prevent leaving his fingerprints on the vial.

I rush to the kitchen. Sergeant Ali, who is busy with Randall, demands to know what I'm doing. I ignore her and sift through the trash with a pair of tongs. Sure enough, amidst the empty snack packaging and pieces of paper towel lies a pair of latex gloves turned inside out, doubtless as Randall peeled them off.

Triumphant, I lift them onto the bench. "You might want to test these for fingerprints."

As Sergeant Ali approaches, I lean closer. A flake of something maroon is attached to the fingertip of one of the gloves. Oh no, I got it wrong!

"Randall's telling the truth. It's not him. It's Bailey." I explain my theory about the vials to Sergeant Ali. "And look—" I gesture to the telltale maroon flake "—this matches Bailey's nail polish."

She frowns. "But what's his motive?"

"Check his parentage. I bet he lied about being adopted. He could be Scarlett's son. And Harry stopped him from connecting with Scarlett."

AN HOUR LATER, we watch from the door as the police car drives down the slippery driveway, taking away another one of our own. When confronted with the evidence, Bailey confessed to murder.

Scarlett and Randall stand apart. She eyes him with distain.

Agnes turns to me. "Will you run any more of these retreats?"

I grimace. "Would you come if I did?"

She smiles. "Absolutely. Wouldn't miss it for the world.

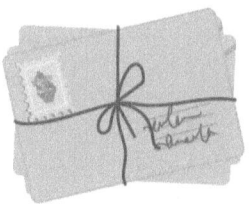

If You Read This, I Have Been Murdered

Gabbi Grey

I STARED AT MY MAILMAN. No, wait, wrong word.

Postal carrier?

Yeah, that was the right term. I might've grown up with *postmen*, and I might be a bit older now, but I could darn well get the right term. I held the yellowing envelope in my hand. "I collect stamps."

The man grinned. "Well, this'll be a new one."

"See this? This is a King George V two-cent stamp. With the 'WAR TAX' on it."

The postal worker, who looked to be barely out of high school, rubbed the back of his neck. "I'm delivering this in person with a formal apology from Canada Post for the late delivery."

I blinked. "Late delivery? This was mailed in 1925. You realize that was one hundred years ago."

"Uh, yes, sir. That's correct."

"Where did you find it?"

"Well, we were doing renovations at the Post Office in Toronto. On Adelaide Street? The place is a museum now.

It's an example of Greek Revival architecture. The building used to be the Fourth York Post Office..."

I cleared my throat.

He blinked owlishly behind thick-lensed glasses. "Right. So, they discovered six letters. This was one of them. Do you know, uh, Margaret MacDougall?"

This time, I blinked. "She was my great-grandmother. She died thirty-five years ago when she was eighty-nine. I barely remember her."

"You musta been young."

I scowled. "I was eight."

"So you're, like, old."

I rolled my eyes. "Forty-four is hardly old."

"My dad's forty-six."

"You're not helping yourself here." Figuring the warning tone would be wasted on him, I simply deadpanned.

He blinked again. "Right. They found six letters they're delivering by hand. We figured Margaret was dead—"

"She would be one hundred and twenty-four."

"Like I said, we figured she was dead. We also figured there was a good chance the people who lived here weren't even related to her."

"Well, there you would be wrong. My great-grandfather, Jeremiah, built this house upon returning from the Great War in 1919. He married Margaret, my great-grand-mother, a year later. Three years after that, my grandfather Daniel was born. He fought in the war to end all wars."

The postal carrier brightened. "World War II, right?"

"Yes."

"Okay, so he fought."

"And returned home. When he married my grandmother, Mary, my great-grandparents moved into a smaller house down the street. Mary and Daniel moved in with my grandparents to take care of them about the time my father married my mother. Jeremiah, Margaret, and Daniel are all dead."

He scratched his nose. "So is your grandmother Mary still alive?"

"Yes, living in that little house. I invited her to move in with me when my parents gifted me this house and moved into a condo down the street, but she likes having her independence. She has a care worker who goes in during the day. I worry about my grandmother constantly, but she assures me she's happy and one day she'll die in her sleep." *And you don't need to know any of that.*

Another blink. "How old is she?"

"One hundred and four."

"Jesus. People live that long?"

I chuckled. "Yes, they do. That's why we still have a few World War II veterans around. My grandmother was a war bride. My grandfather met her while recovering in England from an injury suffered during the war while he was in Holland. They fell in love, married, and she came to Canada. Heck of a train trip from Halifax to British Columbia."

"No planes?"

"Too expensive. Certainly nothing my grandfather could afford on his soldier's pay."

"And she came here?"

"Yes. She arrived before my grandfather and had a huge culture shock. Nothing like the metropolis of London, that's for certain." I held the envelope carefully, worried it might disintegrate in my hand at any moment.

"Well, maybe I should be delivering it to your grand-mother. What's her address?"

I held the envelope away from him. "You've delivered it to the correct address, and I won't be sending it back marked *return to sender*. No, this is the right place. I'll decide what to do with it."

"Right." He bobbed his head. Then he pulled another envelope from his bag. This one was white, crisp, and bore the Canada Post logo. "By way of apology, we have a letter from our customer relations department as well as a book of stamps."

This time, I blinked. "A book of stamps?"

He grinned. "Yeah, the new King Charles III ones. How cool is that?" He handed me the envelope.

"Well, I grew up with Queen Elizabeth II. Heck, I remember her mother."

"Wow, you are old. When did she die?"

"Never mind." I gestured to the door. "Nice to meet you." The *I suppose* was under my breath.

"Yeah. Cool." He took his leave.

I shut the front door, locked it, and headed to the kitchen table. Much of the furniture had been replaced over the years. I'd been quite happy to get rid of my moth-er's pink-rose-on-cream floral-patterned couch. A new mattress had also been in order, but the bedframe remained from my great-grandfather's time. He'd built much of the furniture himself, including this magnificent table. A few scratches over the years, but still quality that stood the test of time.

Who am I going to pass this down to?

I didn't know. I was an only child. My parents had wanted a ton of children, but that'd just never happened.

Growing up in New Westminster had been wonderful. Heck, I'd even gone to Simon Fraser University for my teaching degree so I could stay close to home. My parents gifting me this house had been wonderful, and I still taught at New West Secondary School.

After placing the two envelopes on the table, I set about making myself a cup of pekoe tea. This habit I'd gotten from Nanny. My mother loved her mother-in-law but had never drunk anything but coffee—regular until noon and decaf after that. I'd tried coffee and decided it tasted like a fart. I mean, if a fart had a taste. Just…gross.

Once the kettle boiled and my tea had steeped in a ceramic teapot, I sat at the table. Opening the letter from the head of customer relations was easy. The letter was to the point. 'We're sorry…' Blah, blah, blah. I received even less of an explanation than the overly enthusiastic postal carrier had provided. Just that the letter had been discovered and hopefully, I was able to do something with it.

Right.

I eyed the clock on the microwave. Five o'clock. I did some calculations. Mom and Dad were in Paris for an anniversary trip, so it was way too late to be calling them. Nanny would be finished with her dinner and watching the five o'clock news. Since she always loved when I dropped by —which I tried to do often—I put on my wool coat, boots, hat, and gloves.

Parker, my trusty twelve-year-old Labrador Retriever, poked his head off the couch. He'd slept through the entire postal carrier visit. Back in the day—like a year ago and before—he'd have been jumping up and down for joy at the prospect of a guest. These days, he'd slowed. If my parents came to visit, they got the royal acknowledgment. People clearly not staying? Not worth the effort.

"Do you want to see Nanny?" He moseyed off the couch. My heart clenched. He used to leap off and jump excitedly at the prospect of seeing the one person in the world who gave him unlimited treats. Because of those unlimited treats, I had to watch his diet. I didn't want him to gain weight because that would be hard on his joints.

I put on his light jacket as I didn't want him to overheat, but I also didn't want him to get cold on the walk. Mid-December could be a crapshoot in southwestern British Columbia. Tonight, snow was predicted. Hopefully enough to cancel school tomorrow—although I wasn't holding my breath.

I attached the leash to Parker's collar and we headed out. Again, I locked the door. We walked along Sixth Avenue past Queen's Park. That used to be Parker's favourite place to play, but he didn't pull in that direction anymore. Instead, he kept up a steady pace to Cumberland Street and Nanny's house.

Great-uncle Leonard's letter burned a hole in my pocket. *Am I doing the right thing? Should I read it first?* She'd never met her uncle-in-law, of course. He'd died in 1925 in Toronto, and she'd been born in 1921 in England. Hadn't married into the family until 1945. Came to Canada in 1946.

She didn't talk much about the war. How she'd served as a nurse, tending to wounded soldiers.

Nor did my grandfather discuss his time as a fighter pilot, flying missions over Germany. He'd crashed his plane in Holland. He survived—the rest of his crew hadn't. He walked with a limp for the rest of his life and once, when we'd been alone and I'd been ten, he'd said the bum leg was God's punishment for not saving his buddies. I'd decided that day that God was pretty dumb. I never believed again.

Mother didn't take kindly to that. She and Dad still attended Sunday service without fail. I occasionally joined them for midnight Christmas mass. Mainly if Nanny was up to going. She hated using her wheelchair—used two canes to get around at home—but she'd submit to the *indignity of the chair* to attend church. Truthfully, I questioned whether she believed as well.

Parker peed on Nanny's neighbour's bush. I felt mild guilt because the couple—about my parents' age—always watched out for Nanny. Cleared her sidewalk after the snow fell if I couldn't get there quick enough. If I arrived before they did, I'd do their sidewalk and walkway as well. They certainly weren't getting any younger. I unlocked Nanny's door and entered.

"Leonard? Is that you?" I unclipped Parker, who bolted straight for Nanny.

The snow hadn't started yet, so he was still dry. I'd scented snow on the walk over. *Soon.*

"It's me, Nanny."

"You missed dinner. Pot roast. Leftovers in the fridge. Marta made too much." No admonishment in her tone for her trusty companion—just stating a fact.

"Well, it's like she knew I'd be coming. I stayed late at school and would love some pot roast."

"How's the musical coming?" She sat on her recliner, snuggled in a blanket despite it being about twenty-three degrees in the family room.

I shed my coat. "It's coming together. The show's in

February. I bought a ticket for you as well as Mom and Dad."

"Sounds lovely." She didn't add that she might not be alive then. Occasionally she'd state that. As if she felt she had to remind me that she was a centenarian.

"*Brigadoon.*" I located the pot roast.

Nanny gasped. "My favourite."

I poked my head into the living room. "Hence the reason I chose it." I returned to scooping some of the delicious food onto a plate. I'd spotted her giving Parker one of the special pumpkin treats I'd bought at the Christmas Market last weekend. I set the microwave to cook and got myself a glass of water. "Can I get you some tea?"

"You can heat up this mug. It got cold while I was watching that woman with the hefty chest talking about the storm coming in shortly."

"Nanny." I scolded her as I retrieved her mug. "You shouldn't say stuff like that." I returned to the kitchen.

"Well, she does tell the weather forecast accurately, but that's being fed to her, so it's kind of hard to screw that up."

"Nanny." I pulled the plate with my food out to cool and set about heating up Nanny's chamomile tea. She swore it helped her sleep. Who was I to argue?

"I'm over one hundred years old. If that doesn't give me permission to speak my mind, I don't know what will."

I rolled my eyes as I returned her mug to her.

"You're always such a good boy."

This time, I held in the eye roll. But barely.

I poured myself a glass of water, snagged a knife, fork and plate, and headed into the family room. "Any other news?"

"Vancouver city council is voting on a resolution to try

to deal with the homeless problem. Once the problem was mainly on the Downtown East Side. Now it's everywhere."

I blew on my meat to cool it down. "Affordability crisis. A lack-of-housing crisis. An addiction crisis."

Nanny ran her hands up and down her legs. "After I'm gone, I want you to rent out this house to a family who can't afford anything else. You don't need the money, so don't sell it." We'd had this conversation before. A couple of years ago, she'd had her lawyer draw up a new will, making me her sole beneficiary.

"I can do that." I wouldn't remind her we'd had this conversation at least once a month for years.

Gingerly, I chewed the meat. Ah, perfect temperature. I continued to eat as Nanny channel surfed during the sports segment. She settled on an American cable news station showing an animated anchorwoman discussing the US Supreme Court. Talk about a disaster.

"She's a lesbian."

I almost choked on my peas. "Okay, not that it's relevant. How do you know?"

"I had Marta look her up on Wikipedia for me." She sighed. "My eyesight is too bad."

"I can adjust the settings on your iPad." I was pretty sure the font was set close to maximum, but I was willing to try again.

"It's more the glaucoma than anything else. All good." She flicked back to the Vancouver station for a human-interest story.

I devoured my food. I hadn't realized how hungry I was. The show finished about the time I ate the last bite.

She eyed me. "I can change the channel to the gay man."

I snickered. "He's American, married, and has two kids."

"Doesn't mean he's not eye candy."

"Nanny!" This time, I emphasized the warning.

"I'm just saying—" She smoothed down her blanket again. "How long…?" Her incisive green eyes set upon me.

"Since Lawrence left or since I dated?" I rose with my empty plate and grabbed her empty mug. "Another?"

"Both."

"The answer would be the same." I said the words as I retreated into the kitchen. I was putting the plates in the dishwasher when she spoke.

"Four years is too damn long. Look, the pandemic is over."

I shut the dishwasher, washed my hands, and headed back into the family room. This time, I detoured to my coat. Parker, clearly believing we were leaving, put his snout on Nanny's thigh—asking for just one more treat. She obliged him.

"I didn't say the pandemic was the issue." That had been one of many excuses I'd doled out. Truthfully, I didn't want to bring the virus into this house. We all got our shots and boosters and everything else we could do. For flu as well, and RSV and pneumonia for Nanny. If she were going to die, let it not be from something preventable. I eyed her pill bottles as I sat back on the blue-and-white-delft floral-patterned couch. It reminded her of Holland. England had been her home, but before Hitler, she'd visited the Netherlands frequently. "Have you taken your meds?"

She huffed.

"Do you need fresh water?"

"I need to know what you're clinging to."

Parker, clearly realizing we weren't leaving, positioned himself at Nanny's side. She was a clumsy eater when he was around, and he was happy to eat everything she *accidentally* dropped on the floor.

"It's a letter."

She arched an eyebrow as if to say *duh.*

"It's from Great-Uncle Leonard to Nana Margaret." I'd always called my great-grandmother Nana since I didn't know this grandmother's mother, who'd died in England, having visited her daughter in Canada only once.

"Why would Leonard be writing Margaret?"

"Well, he was her brother-in-law."

"But Leonard and Jeremiah were estranged by 1915. Jeremiah thought Leonard should be fighting in the war. Your great-grandfather signed up the day he turned seventeen, with his parents' permission, and was shipped overseas. He was there for the battle of Vimy Ridge. Almost died."

"Yeah." This story I'd heard many times. If she wanted to repeat it, that was fine.

She pointed to the letter. "What's the date?"

"1925."

"Oh, I was four." Sharp as a tack.

"Yeah."

"Well, there was no sense in him writing to my father at the time—he never spoke of his older brother. Like the man never existed." She pressed a hand to her forehead. "He died in 1925. April, I believe."

I glanced at the postal mark. Still legible and black. "March 31, 1925. York."

"Did you find this at the house? I thought we moved

most of that stuff here. You'll have to take it back after I die, though."

Not looking forward to that. Mom and Dad weren't sentimental so they didn't want anything. It'd be up to me to figure out what could maybe be donated to museums, what should be preserved as family lore—although who I'd give it to, I had no idea—and what could simply be donated, recycled, or thrown out.

"Read me the letter."

"Are you sure?"

"My dear, if you think it's going to impact me now, you can think again. This old ticker's good for another few weeks, at least. Maybe a month or five. I want to see my roses one more time."

I rose and headed to her writing desk, which hadn't been used for that purpose in about ten years. I kept it organized, though, and easily located the ivory-handled letter opener. The envelope opened easily, and I tucked the opener back in the drawer. I headed back to my favourite spot on her couch, removed the folded letter, and met her gaze.

She nodded.

I opened the letter, and my eyes widened after I read the first two lines. I went back to the top and read aloud.

Dearest Margaret,

If you read this, I have been murdered.

I believe that is a tad dramatic, although nonetheless true.

I shall begin again.

Dearest Margaret,

I hope this finds you well. I am sorry we still have not met. Living in Toronto, so far away from you all, is a burden I must bear. I miss my brother Jeremiah desperately, but he is a stubborn man. I will not burden you with the reasons for our estrangement. Perhaps he has already told you? If so, perhaps this letter will be unwelcome. As I could not write to him, I write to you instead. I have no worldly goods to leave behind. As such, arrange to have me buried in a pauper's grave and say a prayer for me. I believe the Lord will not forgive me for my sins, but I may hope.

There is a man who wants to see me dead. A very determined man. Samuel Loughty. I believe he is of no threat to you but if the police inquire, perhaps you may pass along his name. If you read this, he will have murdered me.

I remain your dearest brother-in-law.

Leonard MacDougall.

I stared at the letter. *What the actual…?* Wouldn't do to swear before Nanny, though. She wouldn't appreciate it at all. Parker, whether picking up on some distress or simply seizing a moment, rested his snout on her knee. She grabbed the treats, doled one out, and resealed the container.

"Well…" She frowned. "Obviously, this Samuel Loughty, whoever he is, killed your uncle. Lofty? Odd name."

"L-O-U-G-H-T-Y. I think—" I rubbed my forehead. "I think it might be Irish."

"Well, we'll never know. Or at least if the police caught the man…" She frowned again. "Just because my mother never said anything, didn't mean she didn't know. Murder was rare. Still is rare, I suppose. Relative to the neighbours to the south." She clucked her tongue. "What with everyone owning a gun."

I wasn't even going to attempt to explain that not *every* American owned a gun. Way too complicated and so far from the point of our discussion. "You knew he died."

"Well, yes. There's a date of death entry in the family bible. I assumed Margaret put it there. I asked about him once. This uncle who died in the 1920s. Your great-grand-mother said to never bring him up—especially to your great-grandfather. I discovered that even though your great-uncle was the right age during the war, he never fought. That was the only time I remember him being brought up —when Jeremiah mentioned his cowardly brother not serv-ing. Your dad tried to coax more information, but none was forthcoming."

"Then why am I named after him?"

"Because your stubborn great-grandfather didn't want your father marrying your mother—a Catholic, no less. He and your father fought like cats and dogs for weeks. Jere-miah was uninvited from the wedding and, when you were born a few years later, your father was still pissed. So he named you Leonard. Your great-grandfather lived another two years after you were born. He reconciled with your father on his deathbed."

My eyes widened. "I didn't know any of this."

She snickered. "MacDougall men are stubborn and hold grudges for years. They went almost thirteen years without a civil word between the two of them. Just… ridiculous."

"Glad I'm not that stubborn."

"And when was the last time you went on a date? What about those appy things? Surely you could meet a man and—"

"On that note—" I folded the letter and put it back into the envelope.

"Well, we must track down this Samuel Loughty."

"Come again?" I shook my head.

"We must find out what happened to the man. Surely with that name, there wouldn't be that many in Toronto at the time. The town wasn't all that big back then. Certainly not the thriving metropolis it is today. Traffic's a nightmare."

My grandmother hadn't been to Toronto in over forty years—but she watched *The National* on CBC every night and so got stories from all across Canada. Including one about Toronto traffic, which she'd felt I needed to be warned about.

I hadn't been to Toronto since 2003, when I went to see *The Lion King*. I'd never driven in the city. I didn't even like driving in downtown Vancouver. Who needed the hassle when I could transit downtown to see the Broadway shows that came through town five times a year? Still… "Okay, I'll look him up when—"

"You'll do it right now." She pointed to her desk where her laptop sat. She didn't use it these days, but I navigated around Google when she wanted to know some obscure fact or when she needed help with her banking. She had an email address which I checked once a week. She got more spam than actual emails. I sighed.

Parker rested his snout on her knee. I pointed. "You had dinner before we came. You've had enough." My dog stared until, finally, he gave up. He resettled at her feet.

"You're too hard on the puppy."

"He hasn't been a puppy for about ten years, and the vet said not to let him gain weight." I snagged Nanny's laptop, unplugged it from the power cord then settled back on the couch, put my feet up on the coffee table and turned the machine on.

I waited for her to chastise me about feet on the coffee

table, but she was busy feeding Parker a treat, clearly hoping I couldn't see. Spoiler alert—I totally could.

When prompted, I entered her password. She didn't have anything of great interest on the thing and no saved passwords. In case Marta felt like snooping. And since Nanny kept Marta engaged the entire time the woman was here, that wasn't likely. "Okay." I cracked my knuckles.

Nanny huffed.

Naturally, I only did it around her. I started by searching Samuel's name and Toronto. To say I was startled when I got a hit was an understatement. "Okay, well, I found Samuel Loughty today." I clicked on his LinkedIn profile. "Yummy."

"Drat."

My gaze shot to Nanny.

"Well, I won't be able to see properly."

"He's got blond, floppy hair but professionally cut. High cheekbones and piercing blue eyes. This photo has to be a headshot or something. Good quality."

"What does he do?"

I wasn't certain *this* was the rabbit hole I wanted to go down, but my grandmother would be awake for another few hours and if I wanted to avoid *Wheel of Fortune*, I needed to keep her occupied. "He's a..." I squinted. *Forgot my damn reading glasses. I need to leave a spare pair here.* If I'd known I'd be on her computer, I would've brought them. I was fighting purchasing progressive lenses even though my optometrist was getting pretty militant about me switching over.

"He's a data analyst for one of the big banks. Whatever that means." I searched for him with other social media but couldn't find anything. He might also use a pseudonym, depending on his desire for privacy and his job. Or he might be like me and not be on at all. Well, I had a profile for my students to contact me, but that was strictly professional. Truthfully, I just had no interest.

"Okay, I can send him a message, or——" I squinted. "There's a phone number."

"Well, call him."

"Nanny, I'm certain it's his work phone number, and besides, it's after nine."

"Call him. All the young men stay up until eleven or midnight."

Which made me a very *old* man since I was in bed by ten. Still, I yanked out my cell phone. I had no idea of Samuel's age, although he appeared younger than me. "Are you certain?"

"Yes." She harrumphed.

Humour her. She takes good care of you. She won't be around forever. I dialled.

After three rings, I got a very sleepy, "Hello?"

"God, I woke you. I'm so sorry. I'll call back——"

A low chuckle. "You've got my attention now. Who knows what tomorrow will bring?"

Fair enough. I cleared my throat. "You're Samuel Loughty?"

"Yes." He yawned.

"Any relation to a Samuel Loughty who lived in Toronto about a hundred years ago?"

"Quite possibly my great-grandfather. What's this about?" His voice had lost all traces of sleepiness.

"This is going to sound bizarre."

"I'm all ears."

"My great-uncle mentioned your great-grandfather in a letter."

"A letter written how long ago?"

"One hundred years."

"And you're just getting around to—" He stopped abruptly. "What's his name?"

"Who? My great-uncle."

"Yes." His tone took on some urgency.

"Leonard MacDougall."

"Jesus..."

I blinked. "Uh...that name means something to you?"

"Where are you?" He demanded in an authoritative tone not unlike the one I used with my unruly Grade 9 drama students.

"Uh, New Westminster."

"British Columbia?"

"Yeah."

"Can you text me your address? Where you'll be tomorrow? I'll catch the first—"

"Hold your horses." I chuckled. "You're going to fly all the way out here? Just because of my great-uncle? Are you nuts?"

"I've never been able to track down any of Leonard MacDougall's family. I've been searching on and off for years."

"Were you looking in Toronto?"

"Yeah. I tried casting a wider net, but I couldn't find anything."

"My family's not into genealogy—we know our family trees from way back, and we've had a lot of only children. So not many nosy cousins wanting to suck us in to stuff. We're, uh..." I glanced at Nanny, "...pretty private."

"I need to see you."

"Look, we're getting a big snowstorm tonight. The roads should be clear by Saturday. Why not come then? Better yet why not tell me now?"

"Because I have sensitive information about your great-uncle."

"Yeah, okay. Whatever. I'll text you."

I did. Then I recounted the conversation to Nanny, who was just as baffled. I helped her to bed, then walked Parker home in the falling snow.

THREE DAYS LATER, Samuel J. Loughty sat in my kitchen, nursing a Starbucks Venti coffee and fidgeting. I resisted the urge to still the man's hands.

Finally, he met my gaze. "You…you look so much like him. I mean, the only photo I have is black and white." He pulled a small envelope from his messenger bag.

I took it and carefully extracted the photo. My breath caught. Yes, the photo was monochromatic. But no mistaking Leonard's black hair or his lighter-coloured eyes. "Green? Like mine?"

"That's what my great-grandfather said."

I tucked the photo back in the envelope. "When?"

"1999. He was on his deathbed. He asked to see me. I was all of nine, so it seemed a little ghoulish to me, even then. He gave me an envelope with a written letter and this photograph. He made me swear never to tell."

"Tell what?" The suspense was starting to get to me. I wanted to know what kind of old man swore his great-grandson to secrecy at the age of nine. Or why.

"Why he killed his gay lover." Samuel met my gaze. "Why he killed your great-uncle."

I blinked.

Samuel cleared his throat. "I was named after him. As you were named after Leonard. Have I got that right?"

I nodded.

"Turns out my great-grandfather was, in his words, a 'pansy.' Funny that he might not have told me all this had he known I'd wind up coming out as gay myself."

My mind whirled. I didn't even know how to begin unpacking this. "Uh, me too."

His gaze shot to mine and held.

I cleared my throat. "I guess we might never have the answers."

"Maybe not." He grinned. "But we might have fun searching." Tentatively, he reached for my hand.

I placed it in his. "Yea, I think you're right." In that moment, I saw my future. That made no sense. He lived in Toronto. I lived in New Westminster. Opposite sides of the country. Yet I *knew*.

Turned out, I was right.

The Mystery of the Missing Merchant

Iris March

MOLLY GREEN WIPED AWAY excess soil from the side of a bright pink flowerpot containing a small living stone succulent. Just then, she heard Theo Alexopoulos unlock the front door of Patty's Plant Place. She always spent the first hour of her workday in solitude tending to plants in the staff greenhouse, but the hour had gone quicker than normal that day.

"Good morning," Theo called before she could see him. When he came through the doorway from behind the checkout counter, he hung his zip-up hoodie on the wall-mounted coat rack without looking. Theo had black, curly hair that hung to his ears.

"Good morning to you." Molly moved on to the next pink pot in line, pouring in a small amount of cactus mix soil, and then carefully pulled another living stone from a tray containing the rest of the plants to nuzzle on top of the soil.

"Busy with the succulent subscription boxes this morning, huh?" Theo took in the stainless steel table where

Molly was working. It was covered with supplies and littered with soil.

"Yeah. I got a little messier than normal this morning." She looked behind her to the empty stool where their black and white shop cat sat upright, watching them. "Sherlock's not happy that I wouldn't let him lie on the table."

"I bet he's not." Theo moved around the table and stroked Sherlock's ears. "What can I do to help?"

"I haven't started folding up the boxes yet. Maybe you can start loading them into the boxes to make room on the table."

"I'm on it." Theo moved to the other side of the room and formed the first rectangular box from the flat cardboard. "How many do we need again?"

"Thirty-seven as of this morning."

"That's not bad at all for the second month of doing a plant-through-the mail service. But maybe we need to not work on all of them at once? Send in batches of fifteen or something?"

The front doorbell jingled, announcing May Sato-Flores's entrance. She stood in the doorway between the front of the store and the back room and said in a sing-song voice, "It's succulent box day! How exciting."

"Hey, May," Molly said. She and May were identical twins who looked rather different. Molly wore her brown hair short, while May's hung down her back. Molly wore eye makeup and bright coloured clothing, while May wore blush and lip gloss, and mostly light blue and grey clothing. Molly was shy and quiet, but May was friendly and lost her temper sometimes.

"I didn't print the shipping labels for the boxes yet. I'll do that in a minute." May hung up her own hoodie and left the room with her lunchbox, taking it to the staff break room. Molly had potted one more living stone when she returned. May sat down at the computer desk and began clicking around.

"How was everyone's night? Anything exciting?" May asked, while she typed something into the computer.

"We won the match!" Theo announced. He was on the local minor league soccer team.

"Fantastic!" the twins said at the same time. They smiled at each other because of their jinx.

"I got an assist, not a goal. Hopefully next game." Theo was making quick work of the boxes.

"You'll get one this season, for sure," May encouraged him. "And done. Labels are all printing."

"Thanks, May," Molly said. She slid a few of the potted plants across the table, making room for more.

"Did you want me to start an order for next month?" May asked. "I thought I'd prepare some ads now that we've had our soft launch, and I wanted to have an idea of what might be in the next box."

"So far, I've included two succulents, right?" Molly thought out loud. "One common succulent that I've been growing in the greenhouse, and then something else that we've had to order that's more unique. I hope to grow the more interesting varieties myself eventually but haven't had the time yet. Things take time to grow, after all. The vendor we've been ordering from has been great. These little living stones are top-notch. Why don't you just see what they have that's unusual?"

"Sounds good."

"I've got ten boxes done. Why don't we put some of the pots in here now to clear some room?"

"Wow, Theo." Molly was glad that one part of the succulent subscription boxes went well this month. "That was quick. Thanks."

"We put a sticker on the inside top, right? Where are they?"

"Over here somewhere." Molly stood to show him where the stickers were.

"And don't forget the 20% off coupon for Patty's Plant Place," May said. "Guys, this is weird. I can't find that vendor. Desert Rose Nursery."

"What do you mean?" Molly had located the stickers and handed them to Theo.

"I looked in my email and found the last order. I just clicked on the link at the bottom to go to their website, and it says it's invalid. One of those '404' errors, like it was the wrong website."

"Well, maybe their website is just down. No big deal." Theo pulled the first sticker off the roll.

May shook her head. "There's more. I replied to the email and told them we'd be interested in placing another order. Right away, I got a response saying that the mailbox no longer exists."

The bell above the front door rang, announcing the first customer of the day. "I'll get it," Theo said. "You guys see if you can find the vendor."

"There was never a phone number on their website." May spoke as if to herself.

Molly heard Theo greet the customer who asked about tomato plants. They were almost sold out since it was July, and most people planting gardens in Hawthorn Heights, Ohio, had already gotten their veggies in the ground.

"So, they just closed down without telling their customers? That's too bad. They were good."

"Yeah." May drew out the word, distracted by the computer screen.

Molly shrugged and shoved three plants into their cardboard packaging insert to ensure they wouldn't shift in shipping.

"So, I'm doing a little stalking." May didn't look at Molly as she spoke, clicking away on her mouse. "There's no business listing in the state where Desert Rose Nursery ships from. In Michigan. We chose them because we thought they were close to Ohio. Less carbon emissions and everything."

"Right. But don't all businesses need to be registered?" Molly collected three more plants to transfer to their shipping boxes.

"They should be. And get this." May turned her monitor around to show Molly the screen. "The address for their business that's in my mail? I looked it up on Google Maps. It's an empty lot in Grand Rapids."

"An empty lot?" Molly was dumbfounded.

"It says that the picture was taken last year. They wouldn't have had time to build a new building, probably."

"So what happened? Who's been sending us a shipment of succulents the past two months?" The front doorbell rang, indicating another customer had come in. "I'll see who that is." Molly wiped her hands on her jeans and ducked out the door to the checkout counter.

Harriett Kennedy, a sweet long-standing customer, put her purse on the counter and greeted Molly at the same time as Molly said hello.

"I don't usually jinx anyone other than May." Molly laughed.

"We just know each other well." Harriett beamed up at Molly. Harriett would have been Molly and May's grandparents' age. She knew Patty and Will when they owned the store. "A dear friend just moved into an assisted living facility and, of course, she could use a new house plant to brighten up the space."

"Of course." Molly smiled back at Harriet. "You love people so well, Harriett. What were you thinking of getting for your friend? Any ideas?"

"Something easy to care for that doesn't need direct light."

"Hm." Molly glanced toward their customer greenhouse. "My first thought is a snake plant. Let's go see what we can find." She led the older woman into the shoppable greenhouse. This was one of her favourite parts of the job: pairing the perfect plant with a new caretaker. After some consideration, they selected a hardy rubber plant, and Molly wrapped the plastic sales pot with purple fabric to make it a pretty gift.

"How are your succulent subscription boxes coming along?" Harriett asked as Molly checked her out. There was a poster advertising the boxes behind Molly's shoulder. "I was thinking of subscribing my granddaughter. She loves plants just like her grandma."

"I'm sure she'd love them then." Molly ripped off the receipt and handed it to Harriett. "We send two plants a month, plus a little bonus gift. This month, it's a notepad with a succulent on it. Next month, I'm thinking of a sticker sheet. I might run out of ideas for these little bonus things and have to reuse them. We'll see."

"That sounds lovely, dear. You girls come up with such good ideas."

"It was our cousin Shannon's idea, you know." Molly was excited about the boxes but knew they needed to work out some of the kinks. "And actually, we're having an issue with the vendor we ordered from over the past two months. It's like they don't exist anymore."

"That's odd. It sounds like a mystery to solve, then?" Harriett had a twinkle in her eyes.

"I think it is." Molly chuckled.

After Harriett left, Molly leaned against the counter, took her phone out of her back pocket, and did a search for Desert Rose Nursery. Apparently, there was a garden centre by that name in Arizona. The arid deserts of Arizona made a better location for a desert-themed shop than somewhat humid Michigan, with four of the Great Lakes surrounding it. But this Desert Rose Nursery wasn't a vendor that sold wholesale. It seemed to be a garden centre like Patty's Plant Place. The other search results listed a childcare centre and stores that sold desert rose plants themselves. Molly stepped into the backroom to consult with May again.

"How's it going back here? I have a new mystery clue." Molly was reminded that she still had a lot of work to do on the succulent boxes and sat back down at the stainless steel work table.

May looked up from the computer. "This really is a mystery, isn't it? I found the owner of the vacant lot. It's a real estate holdings firm. I just found the contact info and was going to call. What do you have?"

"I just did a quick search for the vendor's name and found a nursery in Arizona. They're a garden centre like us, not wholesale."

"Do you want to call them too and see what we come up with?" May asked.

"Yeah. You go first." Molly nestled the rest of the potted living stone pots into their cardboard shipping cavities and then set out ten more pink pots to fill with soil, as she listened to May talk on the phone.

May's conversation was rather quick. She talked to a receptionist and then someone else. That second person told her that the land has been in and out of ownership for a few years but had not had a building on it for at least a decade. No business had conducted its work at that location for a long time.

"You heard all of that?" May asked after she hung up the Patty's Plant Place landline.

"Sounds like a truly vacant lot. Weird that any business would claim it as their address."

"Unless it's a shady business," May said quickly.

"But they were such a good succulent supplier. The orders came quickly and were well packaged. The website was easy to navigate. They didn't seem shady."

"That's what makes this so weird. Call that other Desert Rose Nursery. I'm going to see if I can find a new vendor for next month's box." May scooted her desk chair toward Molly and reached across the room to hand her twin the cordless phone.

Molly looked up the number on her phone again and then placed the call. Her heart was beating faster than normal. What time was it in Arizona, anyway? Why was she nervous to call another garden centre?

"Hello. You've reached Desert Rose Nursery."

"Hi. My name is ..."

Our hours are 8:00 a.m. to 7:00 p.m. Monday through Friday and 9:00 a.m. to 8:00 p.m. Saturday and Sunday. It was an answering machine message. *If you've reached this recording, we're either closed or helping another customer. Please leave a message and we'll get back to you as soon as we can. Thanks.*

Molly went back and forth as the recording played, considering whether or not she should leave a message. She decided she might as well and just left her name, Patty's Plant Place, and their phone number. They could call back when they opened.

"They're closed. What time is it in Arizona, anyway?" Molly blew out a long breath.

May clicked around on her computer. "Looks like it's just after 7:00 a.m. there. Kinda early."

"Hopefully, they call back. If not, I'll try again after lunch. Not that we have any idea whether they know anything. They just share the same name."

Molly and May went back to their work. After the new set of ten living stone pots was done and packaged, Molly went to the front of the house and helped a few customers. Theo was busy doing stone and mulch inventory in the backyard. Molly kept wondering about the vendor as she restocked the display of gardening gloves.

Mid-morning, Molly texted her husband, Scott, about the vendor because she couldn't get it out of her head. Scott was a web programmer at a cybersecurity firm in Cleveland. He was working from home that day but didn't reply quickly.

Each of the Patty's Plant Place employees took turns eating their lunch in their small break room. Its dated but not too worn-out furniture reminded Molly of her grand-

parents, especially the plaid loveseat. Before she returned to
the shop floor, Molly called the Desert Rose Nursery in
Arizona again.

"Hello, Desert Rose Nursery. This is Paige. How can I
help you?"

"Hi. I'm Molly Green. I work at a garden centre in
Ohio."

"Well, hello, Molly. Nice to connect with another
garden centre staffer."

Molly was heartened by Paige's friendliness. "We have a
bit of a weird vendor issue going on, and I wondered if you
might know about it."

"Oh, do you think we use the same vendor? Which
one?"

Molly cleared her throat and sat straighter in her chair.
"We've ordered two batches of succulents in the past two
months from a supplier in Michigan that has the same
name as your garden centre. But they seem to have disappeared. We don't know what happened to them. Do you
know anything about another Desert Rose Nursery?"

Paige was quiet on the other end of the line for too
long. Molly listened intently. Had she hung up?

"Molly, I'm sorry I can't help you." However, her voice
did not sound sorry at all. Her tone was defensive and irri-
tated. "We've been getting calls from other people and we
know nothing about that business. It's been a frustrating
couple of weeks and a waste of our time. I suggest you just
find another supplier for your succulents and move on.
Have a nice day." She hung up before Molly could even
thank her or say goodbye.

"So much for that idea," Molly said under her breath to
the empty room.

Theo came into the break room with a sandwich and a bag of chips from the cafe in the neighbouring plaza. "How's it going?"

"I just tried to call that Arizona Desert Rose Nursery again and they don't know anything and don't want to be bothered."

"They weren't nice?" Theo got a glass from the cupboard and filled it at the sink. Then he sat down and unwrapped his sandwich.

"At first, but not when I asked about the vanishing vendor. Oh well." Molly sighed. "Is it very busy out there?"

"No. No one in the shop. May's got the counter covered." He took a huge bite of his sandwich, bigger than Molly would have ever taken.

Molly leaned back in her chair. She supposed she should water some plants or something. She just wished there was some way to find out about their succulent supplier. Then her phone rang. It was Scott.

"Hey, love. Did I catch you on your lunch break?" he asked.

Molly couldn't help but smile at Scott's thoughtfulness. "I was just finishing up. Everything okay?"

"Yeah. I was in video meetings all morning and just saw your text about the succulent supplier who disappeared. Why don't you forward me the email and I'll see what I can do."

"You can help?"

"Well, I work at a cybersecurity company. I write code for firewalls and virus scanners, but other teams at the company also write software to track down hackers. So yeah, I can help." He laughed.

Molly laughed too. "I didn't even think of that. This is

awesome, Scotty! Let me get to the computer." She covered her phone and said to Theo. "Scott says he can help track the vendor by the email they sent."

"He can?" Theo said with a mouthful of chips. He followed her into the other room, carrying his sandwich with him.

Molly sat down at the computer desk, found the email, and forwarded it to Scott. "Sent," she told him. Theo sat down with his sandwich at the work table, still covered in succulent subscription box supplies.

"Alright. Let me put the info into our email analyzer and tracker." Molly heard Scott typing on his computer. A moment went by. "So, this is a bit unexpected. You said this is a company in Michigan that sells succulents?"

"That's right. The return address was from Michigan and that's what it said on their website when it was up. Grand Rapids." Molly found herself nodding along with Theo.

May came into the backroom. "What's going on?"

Theo quietly brought her up to speed.

"I'm going to put you on speakerphone, okay?" Molly asked Scott. He made an affirmative noise. "Theo and May are here."

"Hey, guys. So the address that's coming up is in Grand Rapids, but it's in a residential neighbourhood, definitely not a greenhouse or any sort of commercial building. Our software isn't perfect, but this email doesn't have a lot of encryption. I'd say this is right." Molly heard more typing on Scott's end. She felt giddy. Why hadn't she thought about Scott helping before? "I think I've got a landline number for it. Mark and Donna Thomas. Almost too easy."

"Mark and Donna Thomas. This is awesome."

"Mark and Donna Thomas?" May asked no one in particular.

"Can you reply to the email I sent with the address and phone number?" Molly asked Scott.

"Will do. Tell me what happens when you call. I'm going to walk Watson and eat some lunch before I get back at it." Watson was their fluffy, energetic puppy.

They said their goodbyes and Molly jumped up from the computer desk. "How about that? Seems like this is a real lead."

"But it's not a company. It's a house," Theo said.

"They have to know something, right?" Molly looked between Theo and May.

May nodded in agreement. "I think so. They have to know something. Give them a call. Put it on speaker again."

Molly consulted the email Scott sent, dialed the number and engaged the speaker. She really hoped a new customer didn't walk in right as she was calling. One. Two. Three rings.

"Hello?"

Molly almost jumped. "Hi. My name is Molly Green. I work at Patty's Plant Place. In Ohio."

"Uh. Patty's Plant Place in Ohio?" It was the voice of an older woman.

"Yes. I run a garden centre. Can I ask who I'm speaking to?" Molly tried to sound as friendly as possible. She bit her lip. This lady had no reason to stay on the phone with her.

"This is Donna Thomas. I've never been to Ohio."

"Hi, Donna. We have a bit of a mystery that we think you might be able to help us solve, regarding succulents."

"Oh. I see. The succulents."

"You know about the succulents?" Molly thought she'd have to do a lot more explaining to Donna. And why did the word 'succulents' sound so weird after you said it so many times in a row?

May frowned at her with wide eyes. Theo gave the phone a confused side-eye.

"Well." Donna sighed. "Yes."

"We're looking for Desert Rose Nursery. Do you know it?"

"I do. I suppose you bought some of them. The succulents?"

"We did. They were great. We put them into succulent subscription boxes that were sent to people around the United States." Molly found that she wanted to tell Donna all about how wonderful the succulents were but wasn't quite sure why.

"That's lovely to hear. All across the United States." Donna chuckled. "I suppose I owe you an explanation if you somehow found me."

"We'd really love that. I'm here with my co-workers, May and Theo. We've been wondering why the Desert Rose Nursery closed down so suddenly."

"Hello to May and Theo."

"Hi," the pair said in unison. Theo high-fived May.

"My dear husband, Mark, passed away about a year ago."

"We're so sorry to hear that," Molly said. The others agreed.

"He was a wonderful man. And he loved his plants. We have so many gardens in the backyard. A greenhouse attached to the house. He loved growing vegetables in the summer, but he cared most for his succulents. The green-house was filled with them. Every room in the house had a succulent. Even the bathrooms."

"A man after my own heart," Molly said and put her hand over her heart. She wouldn't have a succulent in every room, but nearly every room in her own house had a plant, including the master bathroom.

"You're very sweet. Well, when Mark died, I couldn't keep up. Our daughter, Maggie, helped, but it wasn't enough. The gardens just aren't thriving under my care. I've actually hired a gardener to honour his memory. I couldn't just let them be filled with weeds and plants that needed tending. The succulents are more resilient, but there are too many. And he was propagating many varieties of them when he died, so now we have even more. We have hundreds."

"Wow. Hundreds." Theo said.

Molly's mind's eye could envision the living stones in Mark's greenhouse. She knew where this was going.

"And so, Maggie helped me set up a company to sell the succulents in bulk. We didn't want to open a shop and just sell a few at a time. We wanted to get rid of them, but we wanted people who could care for them. For garden centres. Like you."

"And we sent Mark's plants on to succulent enthusiasts in our boxes. It's perfect." Molly smiled at her co-workers.

"It sounds like it is. Thank you for distributing them for us."

"But why call the company Desert Rose?" May leaned toward the phone.

"During our travels, Mark liked to go to deserts the most and visit cactuses. Desert roses were his favourite plants that weren't succulents, but we never did make it to Africa." Molly could hear Donna smile.

"And why did you close so suddenly?" Theo asked.

"We simply ran out. I have a few left, but not enough to fulfill bulk orders. Our work is done." Donna's statement held a note of finality. Molly understood that she didn't want to hang on to the past, especially if plants weren't her thing.

"But..." May started to say.

Molly shook her head at May sternly. There was no reason to ask why they didn't tell their customers. Like Donna said, their work was done.

"Well, we appreciate your shedding light on this mystery," Molly said. "And we love Mark's succulents. It's been our privilege to help honour his memory." Even if initially, they didn't know they were doing so.

"I thank you so much for that. Thank you for calling, Molly, May, and Theo from Patty's Plant Place in Ohio. Maggie will be pleased to hear about this." Donna certainly sounded pleased.

They said their farewells and the Patty's Plant Place team sat in silence for a moment, taking in this turn of events.

"That is not how I thought this mystery would end." May finally said. "I thought there'd be a shady company involved. Maybe black market."

"I think we should add a little note to each box this month and tell them about Mark." Molly was already writing the note in her head.

"I think that's a great idea," Theo said. "I need to construct the rest of the boxes. This gives me a lot more enthusiasm to finish them off. For Mark."

"For Mark," agreed Molly. Their new succulent boxes would bring joy to their subscribers but also help another plant enthusiast live on. Molly felt the same enthusiasm as Theo did. Their succulent boxes were more meaningful after this revelation, even if Mark's succulents were no longer in them.

The Road Trip

Albert N. Katz

I WAS SURPRISED to hear a soft tap at my door. Uninvited guests were never good news. I put down my glass of whiskey and my book, and was reaching for the drawer where I keep my revolver when a voice from the past called out, "Jim, you there? I have something weird to show you."

Red hair, scruffy jeans. Veronica Bedlow. The woman who broke my heart.

I was relieved she hadn't brought her chihuahua, Pedro, with her. The two were rarely apart ever since her sister abandoned him when she left. That dog never liked me. Maybe because I never liked his incessant yipping.

She sauntered in, uninvited. "How's everything?" she asked. But she wasn't interested in an answer as she moved around my apartment looking over the books in the wall unit, even peeking into my bedroom. "Not much has changed since you and I..."

Yeah, since you up and left, I thought. "What do you want?" I asked bluntly.

She smiled sweetly. "Whatever you're drinking."

I sighed and poured her two fingers. "Let me put it another way. I was just getting to the best part of the book I'm reading. You know, where the guy who wants to be alone kills the nosy person who disturbs him."

She laughed. It was a pleasant laugh. "Remember my sister, Jessica?"

The question was rhetorical. We both knew it.

I met Veronica when she hired me to find her twin sister, Jessica; the 'witch,' as she put it, who always messed with her head. Always said one thing and did the opposite. The messiest of all her stunts was when she ran off with Veronica's husband, Gary, after saying she couldn't stand him.

Jessica was, well, a million things, none of which involved working hard. Gary had been a scientist at the Environment and Climate Control Agency of Canada until budget cuts led to his reassignment to the ranks of the unemployed. Even then, somehow, he always seemed to scam enough to maintain the lifestyle he preferred and, as Veronica found out, he preferred to keep her sister on the side.

I traced the errant couple to Quebec City. It wasn't hard. They had signed into the Chateau Frontenac as Mr. and Mrs. Gary Bedlow. They had no interest in returning to their former lives, so I took photos, got statements, stuff that Veronica used for the divorce. In the aftermath, Veronica and I became friendly; then, more than friendly. She moved into my condo and all was good until I wanted a wife. She wasn't interested in another husband. End of story. Neither of us had contacted the other in the fourteen months before she showed up at my door.

"Well, and here's the weird thing," she said in an

offhand manner, "I haven't heard from Jessica since she ran off with what's-his-name and I wouldn't be unhappy if I never heard from her again." She reached into her purse and pulled out an envelope. "And yet, here I am with a letter from her."

I just stared at her thinking the less I said the quicker she would leave, I could pick up my book again and pretend she hadn't awakened buried feelings.

"Who knows, Jim? Maybe my ex-husband is now my brother-in-law, and given our past, that would make you—"

"Just the PI who found them."

She smiled wryly. "The odd part is that the letter was sent to my house but it's meant for you, not me. Weird, eh? It may have been sitting in my mailbox since I left for my vacation in Mexico. Two, maybe even three weeks." She handed me the envelope.

It was still sealed. I took it from her and examined it: return address, 61 Frankhurst Street, Lincoln, New Brunswick. Postmarked June 4. Over two weeks ago. Addressed to Veronica's home, as she said, but in a large, scrawled hand across the bottom was added: 'Attention! To Broadbent, James only.' As Veronica said, strange.

"Recognize the handwriting?"

"Oh, it's Jessica's all right. Looks like she wrote it in a hurry, only added your first name as an afterthought, it seems."

My thought as well. Time to call it a day before I said something stupid like 'move back in.' "Thanks for delivering it, I guess. Why not finish your drink and—?" I glanced at the door, hoping Veronica would get the message. She did.

"I'll go when I finish this." She raised her glass.

"Shouldn't gulp down a single malt, I always say. Remember? I like my Scotch with more of a peaty Oban taste," she reminded me, "but this is still good. Talisker?"

That struck home. Not too many people could pick out a Talisker just like that.

She smiled slyly. "My curiosity is piqued. So, while I am sipping away on this fine whiskey," she tapped the glass with the tip of her finger, "why not open the envelope and read the letter?"

I thought for a moment and shrugged. What the hell. Jessica had never been a client of mine, after all. I topped up our drinks.

"We may need this." I handed back her glass, tore open the envelope and extracted a scrap of lined notebook paper:

I'm in trouble and need a PI, and you're the only one I know. Help me Jim.

No signature.

We sat in silence for a few minutes.

"So, what are you going to do?" Veronica asked finally.

"You have her cell number?" I dialled the number she gave and reached an automated message: *The number you have reached is no longer in service.*

"Well, that's that," I said. "I see you've finished your drink."

"What the hell, Jim? She's in trouble! If she needs a PI, she can't call the cops. Otherwise, why send a message to you through me? I wouldn't be surprised if she's into something sketchy. Neither she nor—"

"Gary," I finished for her, "ever turned away from a fast buck."

"You can't just drop this! You know what they say about

twins being psychically connected. Even in Mexico, I had a nagging feeling that she was in danger. This just confirms it!"

"I thought you said that you wouldn't be unhappy if you never heard from her again."

"Don't be a jerk! I'll admit our relationship is complicated, but she is my sister and, hell, if things had turned out differently, she could have been your sister-in-law."

It was a low blow, and it hurt. As if I were the one who wanted out.

"We're taking a road trip," she said resolutely.

"We?"

"Start packing!" She grabbed the envelope from my hand. "We're going to find out who answers the door at 61 Frankhurst Street in Lincoln, New Brunswick. Wherever that is."

PEDRO GROWLED when he saw me and yipped from the back seat whenever I hit a bump in the road. Lincoln was a good four and a half hours away and Pedro yipped often. Veronica had booked us into the Lincoln Suites and Spa because they allowed pets, and she wouldn't leave poor Pedro in a kennel while we extricated her sister from whatever dung heap she had slid into. The place was nothing like the online description: the 'suites' were just regular hotel rooms, spa closed for renovations, no pool. The complimentary breakfast suspended during the COVID lockdown was never resuscitated. True, it was close to the river even if the view of the 'magnificent Wolastoq' was barely visible through the dense foliage. At least the internet and TV worked, the bathroom was clean and the room large enough for Pedro to find a spot distant enough to form a DMZ between him and me.

But there was only one king-size bed. When I raised an eyebrow, Veronica mumbled "the only room available." Like hell! There was only one car in the parking lot and it was ours. I just wanted to find Jessica and bring her home—with or without Gary—in a single day. Cash flow being what it was and me, like a sap, doing the gig *pro bono,* I didn't want to book a second room for the who-knows-however many days it would take to locate Veronica's sister.

Both tired, we slept in the same bed for the first time in much too long, though now separated by a Berlin Wall of pillows.

It turned out that Frankhurst Street was in what was called Hackmatack Gardens, an extensive mobile home community nestled in the greenery of rural New Brunswick, close to the airport and fifteen minutes from downtown Fredericton, the capital city. A perfect location, I thought, for scam artists to make a quick getaway. It also turned out there was no number 61 on Frankhurst Street. In fact, there was no address higher than 20.

"Darn it, Jim! This must just be another one of the ways Jessica is messing with my mind. I'm sorry that she—that I dragged you into this." Then she added dejectedly, "Let's get back to the hotel, pack up and go home." She blushed. "You know, I was hoping that you and I... might... start over. I just... well... I didn't want to be hurt again... after Jessica and Gary."

She wasn't the only one who didn't want to be hurt again. I didn't respond. Instead, I walked to the nearest mobile home and knocked on the door.

"Did you hear what I said, Jim?" Veronica asked as she followed.

"Yeah, I did. We'll talk about it later. Right now, we have to find Jessica, ASAP."

"Jessica. She wins. Again," she said irritably. "Got me to care about her wellbeing and come out on a wild goose chase."

"Look, Veronica, it's no accident that she wanted me to come here. But why? Why the phony address? The way I figure, it must be a clue. I really think she was in danger when she sent the letter. I just hope we're not too late."

I knocked on the door again.

A middle-aged man, scruffy beard, unruly hair, opened the door a crack, just wide enough that I could make out a rifle leaning against the wall behind him. Country and western music in the background.

"Whatchya want?" His eyes moved from me to Veronica, where they stayed as I pulled out the photo of Gary she had given me.

"Have you seen this guy?"

"You a cop?"

"Nope. Just a guy interested in finding him and the woman with him who looks a lot like my companion here."

He glanced quickly at the photo and then his eyes went back to Veronica. "Yeah, he was here. Wanted to check my tap water. I let him take samples like others 'round here done, I understand. Then I called Redmond and told him that these guys had been 'round, and we were finally going to get some action."

"Redmond runs this mobile home park?"

"You don't know nothin', man," he spat. "Redmond runs this place and a lot more. But he's just a cog in a much bigger conspiracy. That's all I's going to say about that."

"If it's a conspiracy, how do you know about it?"

He swore, looked me straight in the eyes. "I keep on top of things that can screw up my life and those 'round me. Been doin' the same since I could shave. I ain't scared of that guy or the thugs he sends 'round. Or you, Mister. Not me. Not like others who live in these here Gardens."

"Do you know where I might find the guy in the photo? Or the woman?"

He didn't answer. He took one last long look at Veronica. "Watch out for yourself, girlie. There's lots of bad people out there," he warned before slowly shutting the door. Then the metallic grind of locks turning reached our ears.

We knocked on the door of every mobile home on that street, and then up and down Hackmatack. Only half answered: retired folks or women with young kids, peeking out from behind their mothers. Most of the residents worked and wouldn't be home until dinner time, we were told. Overall nice people, it seemed. They liked living there. A real community except for the conspiracy nutcase in the first home we had visited and except for a couple of guys down the main road towards the highway who—just rumours, mind you—were into cocaine.

When I showed the photo, we heard a consistent story. The water? Yeah. That man and the woman with him, they came by. Seemed to know that sometimes the water tasted bad. Sometimes mud came out of the tap. Last December we were out of water for the better part of a week. People got sick all the time. Keep calm, we were told, and it'd get it fixed. Boil water advisories about once a month. The guy and the woman took some samples. Said they'd be back, but they didn't. Not a surprise, people lied all the time.

What the residents liked most about living at Hackmatack was that people helped a neighbour in need but otherwise kept their nose out of everyone else's business. Conspiracy nuts and coke heads included.

Redmond? Hadn't seen much of him. He sent guys around now and then. They'd leave Redmond's business card for any new residents and check up on complaints. Nobody complained much. One of the residents flashed the card. I took out my cell phone and snapped a picture of it: Richard Redmond, Lincoln Developments. Fredericton address.

As we drove back to the inaptly named Lincoln Suites and Spa, Veronica said that she felt uncomfortable the way everyone stared at her. I told her to forget it, that they weren't used to seeing beautiful women up in Hackmatack Gardens. She smiled, but I saw in her eyes she was aware that I too had noticed how they all stared. My suspicion was they mistook Veronica for her twin Jessica, and it was as if they were seeing a dead woman walking. But I kept that to myself.

I dropped her off to take Pedro for a walk while I drove into Fredericton to speak to Mr. Redmond. The offices for Lincoln Developments were in what passed for a high rise in the city centre, TD Bank on the ground floor and several commercial enterprises on the upper. I took the elevator to the sixth floor and was met by what we call in my line of business, a gorilla. A muscle man. A fixer.

A voice called out from one of the offices, "Let the gentleman in, Bruno."

Richard Redmond was a balding fortyish-year-old who

looked like he worked out at the gym regularly. He wore a Zegna suit that went for more than I made in a month as a PI. He seemed to be expecting someone. I handed him my card. The pleased look on his face changed instantly to a scowl. It clearly wasn't me he was expecting.

" 'James Broadbent, Private Investigations' What do you want? And make it snappy. I have real business to conduct," he barked as he tossed the card into his wastepaper basket.

There are moments when a half truth is better than a complete lie or total honesty. This was one.

"I've been hired by, well, let's say important people who want to know what happened to employees they sent to investigate environmental conditions at one of the properties you manage." I showed him Gary's photo.

He glanced at it. There was a momentary flash of recognition.

"Never saw the guy! And I certainly haven't received any concerns about water from any of the five hundred or so households in Hackmatack Gardens. Either Bruno or one of my other associates would've heard of any complaints. As for anyone claiming to do environmental assessments, well that's just garbage! I haven't sent anyone out and if someone is doing it, they're just trying to rip off the people who live there."

I casually picked up a business card from the tray next to the lamp. "Lincoln Developments," I read aloud. "Developments in the plural. Are you developing something big out in Lincoln, Mr. Redmond?"

He glared at me, rose from his chair and opened the office door. "Goodbye, Mr. Broadbent. Next time make an appointment!" When I didn't budge, he bellowed, "Bruno!

This man is just leaving." Bruno lumbered in and I made a hasty retreat.

I didn't take the elevator. I took the stairs. It gave me more time to think and by the time I reached street level, several points were clear. First, I hadn't mentioned Hackmatack. He had. So, he lied about the problems the residents were having. The way I saw it, Redmond was a garden variety lowlife who was squeezing what he could out of the folks in the trailer park. And the fact that he recognized the photo of Gary gave me a queasy feeling.

Second, the way Redmond shut me down when I asked about his plans for development indicated something much bigger was in the works than their penny-ante activities at the mobile home park. I couldn't help thinking that Gary and Jessica somehow got between Redmond and his plans, whatever they might be.

All leading to the big question. Was Redmond in this on his own or was he tied in with the man who had a financial stranglehold on much of the province. Bobby 'The Boss' McIntosh was a 'respected' businessman and CEO of the McIntosh Group of Companies. A local mantra went 'what's good for McIntosh is good for New Brunswick.' Those who interfered with what was 'good for McIntosh' tended to fall into line. Or, some say, disappeared. And perhaps Jessica and Gary had crossed that line.

AS WE SHARED a tasty pizza from Franco's Pizza and Poutine on the Lincoln Road, I went over what I'd discovered with Veronica. I left out my suspicions about her sister and Gary. If nothing else, the Lincoln Suites and Spa had good internet connectivity, and we spent the next hours querying 'Redmond,' 'Lincoln Developments,' 'Robert McIntosh,' and the 'McIntosh Group of Companies' for possible clues. We discovered that the environmental assessor used by Redmond at Hackmatack was a firm from the nearby city of Moncton: Geist Consultants.

I was ready to pack it in when Veronica motioned to me from behind her computer screen. She found that a large tract of land adjacent to Hackmatack Gardens was sold for a pittance to an entity called Momentum, owned by one Richard Redmond. One of his business partners in the enterprise was Madeline Boucher, a cabinet minister in a provincial government with no mandatory disclosure of financial holdings. And the assessors hired to confirm that the leased tract of land was safe for development were from Geist Consultants, the same assessors who turned a blind eye to the water problems in the adjacent trailer park.

Further searches pulled up an exchange in the provincial legislature where a member of the opposition had asked Minister Boucher about the status of a residential development and shopping centre near the Fredericton airport. The minister responded that the people of that area sorely needed housing, that the proposed development would help revive the moribund local economy, and that the government was poised to fast track the proposal.

A nice witch's brew I thought—big plans, a questionable project, and a government minister.

The next step was to arrange a meeting with Madame Boucher. Her staff was reluctant to grant me one until I carefully pointed out that I was investigating the disappearance of two people and that she might have valuable information. My appointment with the minister was scheduled for a thirty-minute slot at 3:00 p.m.

Madame Boucher looked to be in her mid-thirties, surprisingly young for someone in her position. One of the up-and-coming stars in the government, she was athletic, energetic, enthusiastic, and perfectly fluent in both of New Brunswick's official languages. But her enthusiasm waned the instant I brought up the reason for my visit: her non-disclosed financial interests in a development on land leased from Robert McIntosh and managed by Redmond, a low-grade grifter, if ever I had seen one.

She was feisty. How dare I question her integrity! Mr. McIntosh was a respected businessman, a pillar of society. Mr. Redmond was an upstanding member of the community. She would, of course, declare a conflict of interest when the matter came up for a vote! Her show of righteous indignation was topped off by a threat that she would see me in court if I made any scurrilous claims in public.

Her confident harangue ended quickly when I asked if part of fast-tracking the project was pushing through environmental assessments by a hand-picked firm used by Redmond, maybe before declaring her conflict of interest. And, oh, by the way, I wondered, could a proposal for a residential development and a shopping centre proceed if an independent assessment demonstrated the leased land was environmentally contaminated? I showed her Gary's photo. He had done an independent environmental assessment, I pointed out, but he and his associate had since disappeared. Did she have any idea what had happened to them?

Caught off guard and visibly shaken by my barrage of questions, she abruptly terminated the interview. I left with the sense that she was surprised by all I had revealed; she looked like a deer in the headlights.

Veronica and I agreed. With Boucher's unwitting backing, Redmond planned to build on land that wouldn't pass a legitimate environmental assessment. But by using the old faithful Geist Consulting, that obstacle was easily overcome. At least until Gary and Jessica had stuck their noses in. My bet was that Gary documented the environmental problems and then went to Redmond to negotiate his silence in return for a substantial contribution of money. It was what a two-bit con artist would do. But it seemed to me that Redmond wasn't the kind of guy who was open to negotiations.

"What do we do next, Jim? We have a cohesive story, but nothing concrete we can bring to the police."

I thought back over everything from the instant Veronica had entered my condo with the letter. The way she described how her sister messed with her head by saying one thing and then doing the opposite. The fake address. The odd way my name was written on the envelope.

Then came the eureka moment. It was so obvious. "Let's take a short drive. And bring Pedro."

Veronica looked surprised. "Pedro?"

"Pedro," I repeated.

Frankhurst Street, the clue that led us there in the first place. I parked the car outside mobile home number 16, the first we had visited. Once again I knocked, and the door opened a sliver. Not too wide but enough for Pedro to rush inside.

A woman's voice cried out in delight, "Pedro!"

The man opened the door wider, looked around to

make sure we were alone and shrugged. "Might as well come in. I'll put up a pot of tea."

Dressed in faded, torn overalls, Jessica was stretched out on the black faux leather couch with Pedro wriggling ecstatically in her lap. I could see a room filled with electronic equipment down the hall. Jessica looked like the cat that ate the canary.

"See, Franklin?" she said to the man pouring water from a large plastic jug into the kettle. "I told you Veronica would come and bring Jim with her!" She sat up, put Pedro on the floor and turned to her sister. "Thanks for coming to find me. I wasn't sure... didn't think you'd ever want to help me after..." Then she whispered, "I'm so sorry." She looked at us both. "You two always looked so right together. I was hoping you'd be able to work together and figure out that I reversed your name on the envelope, so you'd reverse the number in the address from 61 to 16."

Veronica was exasperated. "Why didn't this guy"—her thumb pointed to the man setting the kettle on the burner— "let us in when we were here earlier?"

"This guy, as you put it, is Franklin, the man with whom I've fallen in love. I thought we should have let you in but he's a cautious man," she explained soothingly, "a very loving and protective and careful man." She beamed at him.

To my astonishment, Franklin prepared the tea in a porcelain teapot and after it had steeped for exactly three minutes, poured it into fine china teacups. He nodded at me. "You can't be too careful. Redmond has half the cops 'round here in his pocket, and I didn't know if you were in his pocket, too. And I knew that Jess's sister was angry with her for running off with her husband, so," he said looking at Veronica, "I wasn't sure I could trust you either. I checked around after you guys left and found out that you were really looking for Jess, but well, old suspicions die hard! Jess is helping me overcome that."

"What happened, Jessica?" I inquired softly.

The story she told was much as Veronica and I had worked out. Once the environmental data had been compiled, Gary went to see Redmond to shake him down. Jessica didn't want any part in the scheme but, you know, the money sure sounded good. She was supposed to meet him at the variety store on Hackmatack Drive after he spoke to Redmond, but, well, things didn't work out as he had planned. She was waiting at the store when his car came speeding down the road toward the highway, closely followed by two others in hot pursuit. Gary didn't stop to pick her up, and, well, she hadn't heard from him since.

"I 'spect they just wanted to get their hands on the data he collected and when they caught up with him, they beat the heck out of him. Gary'll be laying low for a long, long time. In any case, he's gone, and Redmond's men'll have a description of the woman helpin' him. They'll want her silenced, too," Franklin added.

"How did you get involved?" I asked.

"I was in the store at the same time and saw what happened. Jess was so scared. Well, I brought her back here. She told me everythin'. Not that I was surprised." He pointed down the hall to the bank of electronics. "I monitor everythin' Redmond does. I knew McIntosh wanted to get some sucker to buy the land contaminated by the old gasoline storage site he once had there next to the airport. He didn't want to pay the millions needed for the environmental clean-up. Redmond was that sucker, and once he found out the land was contaminated, he knew he'd go bankrupts trying to clean it up. So, he tried instead to get a phony assessment done to get the project built."

I nodded. "And Jessica?"

"Redmond's men came 'round as I 'spected, but people hereabouts help one another and don't put their nose into other people's business. Good people. Some on the street know she's here, but no one'll blab. Like I said, good people."

"What on earth—" Veronica blurted but I interrupted.

"You have Gary's data, don't you, Jessica? That's why you sent the letter. You want me to get it to the right people."

She nodded. "Whatever Gary's shortcomings, screwing around, abandoning me to Redmond, well, all this shouldn't be for nothing" she added ruefully.

Veronica took a deep breath. "Come and stay with me until you figure out what to do next."

"That's nice, Sis, but I like it here. Me and Franklin like the simplicity of the place. The air around here feels new and fresh. As Franklin said, good people. And you know, he's a good man. He knows how to use that equipment of his. Made a few million in bitcoin. We plan to winter at his villa in Italy." She beamed at him. "I've even developed a taste for country and western music."

Veronica and I sat quietly in shock at the news and just drank our tea.

BACK HOME, I made copies of Gary's data and wrote out everything Veronica and I had discovered about the proposed development. I named names, filled in as much as I could, including a description of Gary's car. Maybe he's hiding out in a shack somewhere. Maybe, like Franklin said, he'll never be found.

I sent copies to everyone and everywhere that mattered. You name it, they had a copy. There is enough in what I sent out to ensure that it makes the news and gets the police to sniff around. Maybe they'll nail Redmond; maybe not. In any event, there's enough there to make sure a proper environmental assessment is carried out. The development is certain to be put on hold. Indefinitely with a huge financial cost to the players involved. I doubt if anyone will pay to clean up that plot of land in my lifetime. But I won't feel sorry if Redmond goes broke, and I suspect Minister Boucher's rising career in politics will take a dive. Innocent dupe or not, she had at the very least demonstrated poor judgement.

Veronica comes around frequently these days, sometimes stays over. I bought some single malt Oban for those occasions. We've had that talk about getting back together. I think it will work this time, especially since the twins agreed that Jessica could keep Pedro. It was her dog first after all, and he'll have a lot more space to run around in Hackmatack Gardens or in the villa in Italy than cooped up in our condo. And I won't have to listen to his constant yipping.

The Tiffin-Box Thief of Rue des Jasmins

Rachel Desiree Felix

SNOW DUSTED the iron railing outside her apartment like powdered sugar. Divya Ravindran climbed the steps slowly, boots soaked from the slush, arms aching from the double shift at the eldercare centre. Verdun's December light had long faded, and even the streetlamps seemed half-hearted. She reached the landing and paused. A brown-paper package sat by her door.

No Canada Post sticker. No forwarding address. Just her name—almost.

D. Raveenathan

Close, but not quite.

She bent down. The package was about the size of a shoebox, tied with brown string in small, perfect knots. Someone had wrapped it with care. Not the rushed care of a courier, but something older. Familiar. The kind of wrapping you learn from habit, not instruction.

She checked the hallway. Empty. No footsteps. No neighbour's door ajar.

Inside, beneath two layers of Tamil newspaper, was a

stainless steel tiffin-box—small, old-fashioned. Three compartments, each slightly misshapen. Scratches mapped across the surface like ghost roads. When she opened the lid, a faint scent rose up—turmeric, dried chili, the sharp tang of tamarind that clung even after years of washing. Something snagged in her throat. The smell tugged at her chest—sharp and sudden. Not quite a memory, not quite grief.

Meena's tiffin-box had a dent like that. She shook her head. It couldn't be.

Still, she carried it inside, boots dripping at the threshold. She peeled off her coat and scarf, setting the parcel on the counter. The heater clanged in the corner like a forgotten bell.

As she washed the tiffin-box at the sink, her fingers worked automatically. Scrub, rinse, dry. Muscle memory. She polished the lid with a dish towel, noting the oval dent at the base—familiar in a way that made her stomach tighten.

For a moment, she considered tossing it. But she placed the tiffin-box on the kitchen shelf instead. There was something indecent about throwing it away.

Outside, snow fell heavier, blanketing the alley between apartment blocks. Across the way, a neighbour was stringing fairy lights, their reds and greens blinking faintly behind frosted glass.

Divya opened her cupboard and reached for incense. A stick of *nag champa* tonight. She lit it and touched her fingers briefly to the photo on her bookshelf—an old Polaroid, faded but intact. Two girls in school uniforms stood knee-deep in seawater, hair windblown and grinning. She didn't pray. Not anymore. But she bowed her head. "For you," she whispered.

Dinner was quiet—leftover *dal*, plain rice, pickled onions from a jar she'd brought from Malaysia. Comfort food.

Later, she sat in bed wrapped in two layers of blankets. The pipes gurgled behind the walls. Upstairs, someone moved—a slow step, a sigh. She turned on her side and stared at the tiffin-box. The name on the parcel. Not hers—but not a stranger's either. Close enough to be unsettling. Too strange to ignore.

The next morning, she brought the empty package to the recycling bins by the side stairwell and ran her fingers over the paper. There was no print on the inside—just Tamil script from a torn newspaper. She didn't recognize the date, but something about the layout felt...old.

Back upstairs, she searched the string knots again—tight, symmetrical. Practised. Not store-bought twine but kitchen-grade. Jute. South Asian grocery type. She grabbed a notepad and wrote: *Tiffin-box. No label. Name misspelled. Hand-delivered. String = jute. Tamil newspaper. Unknown date.*

Then, beneath it: *Ask Kavitha Aunty? She knows all the aunties.*

She didn't call yet. But the thought of calling stayed with her as she washed her breakfast cup and stared out the frosted window. Someone had left her a message. Maybe more than one. She just had to learn how to read it.

———

THE SECOND PACKAGE arrived three days later.

Smaller this time—no bigger than a paperback—and

wrapped in the same brown paper with the same looping string. It was lying on the mat outside her door when Divya came home, perfectly centred. She stood there a moment, boots dripping slush onto the concrete, pulse thudding.

The name read: *Miss Anitra R.*

Again, not quite right. But closer than before.

She picked it up slowly. Same twine. Same crisp edges. Still no postage, no stamp, no barcode. Not mailed—delivered. Again. Inside: a folded bus ticket. Worn, water-stained, corners curled.

Penang → *KL Sentral*

The date, faint but legible: *12 March 1999.*

Her fingers trembled. That trip. That exact ride.

She and Meena had gone to visit their grandmother after a fight with their mother. Silent for most of the journey. But somewhere near Tapah, Meena had passed her a pack of *kacang putih*—her version of an apology. She never used words when food could do the job.

Divya held the ticket up to the light. The paper had a yellowed transparency, as if aged in sunlight. She laid it gently beside the tiffin-box on the shelf above the stove.

Two strange arrivals now. Two near names. Two parts of a puzzle she hadn't meant to start solving. But someone clearly wanted her to.

THAT NIGHT, she stood by the window, arms crossed, watching the lights flicker across the alley. Her reflection hovered faintly in the glass—hair unbrushed, jaw tight. She retrieved her notebook from the kitchen drawer. *Second pack-*

age. Bus ticket from 1999. Date: March 12. Personal relevance: yes.
Origin unknown. Name = Anitra R.

Beneath it, she drew a faint timeline:
- *Sunday — Package 1 (Tiffin-box)*
- *Wednesday — Package 2 (Bus Ticket)*

Both in the evening. Both wrapped by hand. She circled
a question: *Is someone watching the building?* The thought gave
her pause. But the feeling it stirred wasn't fear—it was more
like an ache. Someone remembered this. She stared at the
name again: *Anitra.*

That wasn't a common typo. That was someone who
remembered how Meena used to call her Annie sometimes,
when they were small. Annie Ravi. A mash of nickname
and last name. She closed the notebook and lit a stick of
sandalwood incense. Just to fill the air with something
warm.

Her phone buzzed on the table. A text from Maxime,
the clerk from the post office across the street—a reminder
about her mail-forwarding form. She stared at the screen,
thumb hovering, then typed:

> Hey, random question. You ever seen
> anyone leave a package at my unit? No
> postage, just placed by hand.

Three dots appeared.

> Not that I noticed—but I'm only at the front
> from 9–3. Some of the neighbours use the
> side stairs, though. Why? Something
> missing?

Divya hesitated.

> Not missing. Just…unexpected. Will
> explain sometime.

She deleted the message before sending. Instead, she texted:

> No worries. Thanks anyway. :)

She set the phone down, then looked back at the shelf. The tiffin-box and the ticket. She added one more note to her pad before bed: *Ask at Tamil temple. Old donation drives. Lost property boxes?*

If these things weren't from Canada Post, someone had to be *carrying* them. Someone who knew her well enough to trace the quiet spine of her past.

TWO DAYS LATER, another package.

The snow had hardened into sheets, squeaking under her boots as she climbed the front steps. A brittle cold—one that bit through gloves. The parcel waited for her like before. Nestled neatly at the door. Wrapped in newspaper this time, edges tucked in like a carefully folded sari.

The name read: *D. Ravinran.*

Fewer letters. Even less correct. But something about it made her chest tighten. She crouched and touched the wrapping gently. Tamil script again—this time from a *Tamil Murasu* page about temple closures in 2015. She only recognized it because her mother had once mailed her that same article.

She carried the package inside, setting it down beside

the tiffin-box and bus ticket on the shelf. Then, slowly, she unwrapped the paper. Inside: a half-used tin of Baba's fish curry powder. The yellow lid was taped shut, and a strip of masking tape crossed the bottom. She shook it. The sound was familiar—soft, solid clumps thudding inside like a heartbeat. She peeled the tape and opened the lid. The scent was immediate. Fenugreek. Chili. Coriander. And a hint of tamarind, sharp and sour. She turned the tin over. *Expired: May 2017*

Her heart beat faster.

She hadn't used this brand in years. She used to smuggle a few tins back from Malaysia in her suitcase, tucked between socks and plastic bangles. Montreal didn't carry this specific blend—too niche, too regional. Meena used it too. Always too much curry powder, never enough salt. She held the tin with both hands and closed her eyes.

A memory rose—uninvited and clear. The two of them in that rented apartment near Chow Kit, twenty-two and broke, laughing as onions sizzled in coconut oil. Meena barefoot, humming out of tune, arguing about how much *asafoetida* to add.

Then—just static. Years of silence.

She opened her notebook again and added to the list:

• *Friday — Package 3 (curry tin)*
Newspaper = Tamil Murasu (2015)
Item = Baba's curry powder (expired 2017)
Name = D. Ravinran

Then, she underlined: *Not from store. From storage? Donation bin? Temple kitchen?*

Her gaze moved from the tin to the tiffin-box. Three objects now. All distinctly hers—or Meena's. Each wrapped with intention. Not garbage. Not random.

She flipped back in her notebook to an earlier entry: *Ask Kavitha Aunty.* She underlined it twice. *Tonight*, she promised herself. *After work.* But before she left for the eldercare centre, she opened her laptop and typed: *Meena Ravindran.*

Nothing useful appeared. A few obituary databases, a link to a ten-year-old blog on South Asian feminism with a broken profile image.

She tried *M. Pavadai*—that had been their mother's maiden name. One Facebook profile: private, no photo. Last activity, 2016. Location, Montréal. She clicked. Nothing but the default silhouette. She leaned back in her chair. Closed the lid.

The apartment felt too quiet again. Just the hum of the fridge and the whine of radiators.

She lit another stick of incense—jasmine this time. Just to breathe something other than questions. Then, gently, she arranged the three items on the shelf above the stove. Together, they looked like an altar. Or a riddle. And still— no note. No return address. Just the feeling that something, or someone, was trying to be remembered.

THE FOURTH PACKAGE arrived on a Sunday morning.

Overnight, the snow had softened into deceptive quiet. The city felt suspended. The parcel was propped gently against her door—balanced, never tossed. As if placed with care.

The name read: *D. Raveendran.*

Closer than it had ever been. Almost correct.

Her hands shook as she picked it up. Inside: not paper. Not string. Sari fabric. Faded and soft, patterned with block-printed florals. She unfolded the cloth slowly, hands reverent. Tucked inside was a torn sheet of school notebook paper—frayed at the edges, thick with age. Tamil script ran across the top in tight, slanted lines.

Thangachi, it began.

Little sister.

I'm sorry about your sister. She never forgave herself.

No signature. No date. But her breath hitched. That word—*Thangachi*—landed deep. She ran her thumb over the edge of the page. The writing looked hand-formed, not printed. The sort of penmanship taught in small village schools, with rulers and red marks. She couldn't read Tamil fluently. Only letter shapes. A few words here and there. But she knew sorrow when it bled through paper.

She wrapped the note back in the sari cloth and folded it into her coat pocket. There was only one person she trusted to read this without embellishment. *Kavitha Aunty.*

The walk to her shop was slow, the slush thick and clinging. Every few steps, Divya glanced over her shoulder, not out of fear, but anticipation. The bell above the door chimed as she entered. Heat greeted her with the scent of turmeric, basmati rice, and fried *murukku.* The aisles were narrow and overfilled. Jars of pickles. Binders of spice packets. Stacks of VHS films no one had rented in a decade.

Kavitha looked up from behind the counter.

"Divya! You look pale, ma. Come, sit down."

Divya didn't answer right away. She stepped up and slowly unwrapped the sari cloth. She laid the note on the counter.

"Can you read this?"

Kavitha adjusted her glasses. Her fingers hovered over the page, not touching, just sensing.

"Hmm," she murmured. "This handwriting—I know this. Very tidy. Chitra. Yes, yes. Chitra R."

Divya's voice cracked. "Who is Chitra?"

"Quiet girl," Kavitha said. "Used to live above the old Tamil temple on Rue des Jasmins. Volunteered at food drives. Helped sort donations."

Divya's notebook was out before she noticed. She scribbled: *Chitra R. Temple volunteer. Address: Rue des Jasmins.*

"Did she know Meena?"

Kavitha paused. "Yes. They were...close. Meena helped her with English letters. Grocery runs. They laughed together. Not just neighbours."

Divya folded her arms. "Was Chitra connected to the post office?"

Kavitha's brow furrowed. "Part-time, I think. Back-end sorting. Not official staff. But she handled paper like it was sacred. Said it helped her remember what people forgot."

Divya looked down at the note again.

I'm sorry about your sister.

"Did she leave a forwarding address?"

"No. Disappeared maybe three, four years ago. Before she left, she told me she was cleaning out storage from the temple—old tins, letters, forgotten parcels. Wanted to return things."

Divya swallowed. *Return things.*

That aligned with everything. The tiffin-box. The bus ticket. The curry tin.

"You're sure this is her handwriting?"

Kavitha didn't answer with words. Instead, she opened the drawer beneath the till and pulled out an old, laminated name tag. *CHITRA R.* in black ink, beneath a faded temple logo.

"She left this here," Kavitha said softly. "I kept it. Not sure why."

Divya pressed her fingertips to the name.

"Thank you," she whispered.

Kavitha slipped a small bundle of fresh coriander into Divya's tote. "On the house. Something green for your mystery."

Outside, the wind stung Divya's face, but she hardly noticed. Her mind moved quickly now. *If Chitra was sending the packages…and she worked at the post office…*She reached for her phone. Maxime. He'd know if the post office had any record of her.

The post office on Rue de l'Église was wedged between a Korean fried chicken place and a laundromat. From the outside, it looked like it hadn't been updated since 1984. Frosted glass windows, a faded red sign, and one side of the door permanently jammed.

Divya stood outside, scarf tucked to her chin, tote bag heavy against her shoulder. Inside the bag: the tiffin-box, the folded note from Chitra, the expired curry tin, the bus ticket. The bell jingled as she stepped in.

Warmth wrapped around her—radiators humming, ink and toner sharp in the air. Maxime stood behind the plexiglass divider, rearranging a stack of prepaid envelopes. He looked up and smiled.

"Bonjour—oh! Divya, right? Bird stamps, if I remember correctly."

"That's me." She smiled, then hesitated. "Do you have a few minutes?"

"Sure. What's up?"

"I'm trying to find someone who used to work here. Or volunteer. Her name was Chitra R. Tamil. Quiet. Maybe around 2020 or so?"

Maxime tilted his head. "That name does ring a bell. Give me a sec."

He tapped at the computer, squinting behind his glasses.

"She wasn't full-time staff. But I'm seeing her name on a few community bin reports."

Divya leaned in. "Community bin?"

"Yeah, we used to have this volunteer program—mostly retirees and students. They'd help sort undeliverable or unclaimed mail. Stuff from deceased tenants, shut-down PO boxes, unlabeled parcels. Some of it got redistributed to shelters or repurposed for donation drives."

He scratched the back of his neck. "Temple kitchens loved tins. We got a bunch during the temple consolidation years. You'd be surprised how many people donate lunch boxes."

Divya reached into her tote and pulled out the tiffin-box.

"Like this?"

Maxime blinked. "Yeah. Exactly like that. Three-tiered stainless steel? That was one of the most common types. Durable and easy to clean."

He paused. "You said her name was Chitra?"

Divya nodded. "Did she log what she took?"

"Not formally. But wait—" He disappeared into the back, then returned with a thick blue binder.

"Volunteer sign-in sheets. If she signed anything, it'll be here."

Divya flipped through the pages at the side counter.

The sheets were in both English and French, with dates, initials, sometimes notes.

There—toward the end of 2021. *Chitra R.* — *Rue des Jasmins.* Written in the same tidy script as the note.

Maxime leaned over. "She was here a lot. Weekly, sometimes twice."

"She didn't list items taken?"

"Just checkmarks. But…"

He pointed at a column labeled 'Type.' Next to several of her entries: *TIN, LETTERS, PHOTOS.*

Divya circled them softly with her fingertip.

"She was leaving them," she murmured. "Piece by piece."

Maxime raised an eyebrow. "You think she's the one who's been delivering them?"

Divya nodded. "Not mailed. No postage. No stickers. Just…placed."

Maxime looked thoughtful. "We never had complaints about her. She was careful. Almost reverent. Like she believed these things still had stories to tell."

Divya closed the binder. "They do." She reached into her tote again and pulled out the folded note.

Maxime didn't read Tamil, but he studied the paper. "Same hand. No doubt."

"Any way to contact her?"

Maxime shook his head. "I think she moved. No forwarding address. She just…stopped showing up."

On the corkboard behind the staff counter hung a row of lost and unclaimed items: children's drawings, orphaned postcards, an old family photo. Divya stared at one—three women in saris on a Montreal rooftop, one of them laughing, her head tilted in the sun.

Her breath hitched.

"That's her," she said softly. "The one in the middle."

Maxime looked, then back at Divya. "Want to take it?"

She didn't answer. Not yet. Instead, she reached into her notebook and wrote: *Chitra R. worked weekly. Volunteer. Retrieved tins, letters, photos. Left quietly.* Divya underlined: *Returning what was never claimed.*

When she left the post office, her tote bag felt heavier. Not from the weight. From the knowing.

THE FIFTH PACKAGE arrived on a Monday evening.

There was no knock. No footsteps. Just a hush outside the door and a familiar weight resting against the frame— like someone had leaned in gently, then disappeared.

Divya paused before reaching for it. The paper was different this time—white, slightly wrinkled, the corners tucked rather than tied.

And the name: *D. Ravindran*

Spelled right. At last.

She carried it inside like a fragile offering. Sat cross-legged on the floor. She peeled back the paper slowly, almost ceremonially. Inside: a black-and-white photograph. Three young women stood on a rooftop in Montreal, their saris caught mid-billow in the wind. The photo had aged— creases like old riverbeds—but the women's faces were clear.

The one on the left laughed with her head tilted back. The one on the right threw a peace sign. The woman in the middle—short hair, crooked smile, hand shading her eyes— was unmistakably Meena.

Divya's throat tightened. It was a version of her sister she hadn't seen in years. Not guarded or careful. Just being.

Tucked behind the photo was a folded letter, in English this time. She unfolded it with slow hands.

Divya,

I found these things in Meena's storage box when I helped clear out the youth cenrte archives. She always meant to write to you. I waited. But when she passed, no one came. No one knew who to call.

She used to cook for the kids. Said rice and dal could fix almost anything. I think she believed that if she kept feeding people, she might one day feel full again.

I didn't know how else to return what was hers—what might still be yours.

I'm sorry it took me this long.

Chitra

Divya pressed her fingers to the words. The page smelled faintly of sandalwood and something older—dust, maybe. Or quiet. The heater clanged behind her, the pipes knocking in reply.

She rose and placed the photo beside the tiffin-box, the curry tin, the bus ticket, and the sari-wrapped note. Then she gently folded the letter and slipped it into the middle tier of the tiffin-box. An offering returned. A message received.

Later, she made rice. Simple *dal*, tempered with mustard seeds and curry leaves. No chili. Meena always said spice wasn't proof of strength. She hummed a lullaby their grandmother used to sing during monsoon blackouts. Meena had hummed it, too—absently, while folding laundry or stirring tea.

She sat by the window to eat, each bite deliberate. Outside, snow whispered against the glass.

Then she picked up a pen and wrote her own letter.

Meena,

I'm sorry we stopped talking.

I thought I had more time to fix it.

But thank you for sending me home in pieces.

Love,

Divya

She folded the letter and tucked it into the tiffin-box, alongside Chitra's. Closed the lid gently. Not locked. Not sealed. Just held.

The shelf above her stove had become something sacred. A shrine, maybe. Or just a reminder that memory isn't linear. Some stories don't arrive all at once. Some are delivered—quietly, faithfully—until we're ready to open them.

THE SNOW BEGAN to melt by the second week of March. Just enough sun had broken through the clouded sky to loosen the ice at the curb outside Divya's building. The light lingered longer now. It filtered through her kitchen window like a soft forgiveness. She no longer paused at the door, expecting packages. But some mornings, she still glanced—just once—before turning the key.

The shelf above the stove had settled into its role.

A tiffin-box, sealed but not locked.

A folded bus ticket.

A yellowed photo.

A tin of curry powder, long expired.

Together, they told a story. She didn't explain it to visitors. When friends came over, they assumed it was nostalgia. An immigrant's sentimental collection. No one noticed the middle compartment of the tiffin-box was always left empty. No one asked why it was always clean.

AT THE YOUTH shelter near the old Tamil temple, she introduced herself as Meena's sister.

The director—an older man with kind eyes and mismatched socks—looked up sharply.

"She was one of ours," he said. "Quiet, but she showed up every week. Always brought food. Said it helped her feel useful."

In the kitchen corner, some of the kids still called it *Aunty Rice*—a simple meal Meena used to bring in warm tiffin-boxes, always with extra pickle. One child asked if Divya knew how to make it.

She smiled. "I'm learning."

In the back storage room, beside rolled-up sleeping mats and outdated posters, there was still a box labeled *M. Ravindran*. Inside: a folded shawl, two recipe books, a bar of Mysore sandal soap, and a small notebook filled with meal plans scribbled in Meena's messy, hopeful handwriting.

Divya didn't take the whole box. Just the soap.

That night, she unwrapped it and let the scent bloom in her bathroom—woodsy, warm, familiar. Grief still came. Some days, heavier than others. But it no longer hollowed her. It shaped her.

SHE BUMPED into Maxime near the recycling bins outside the post office one Friday evening.

"Been thinking about your mystery," he said.

She laughed. "Still?"

"Sure. But maybe it wasn't a mystery at all. Just something waiting to be seen."

She nodded. Not in agreement, but in understanding.

That April, she mailed a small parcel to a Tamil community archive in British Columbia.

Inside: a scanned copy of the rooftop photo, a translated version of Chitra's letter, and her own note: *Some stories go unspoken for too long. But silence is not the same as forgetting.*

In her apartment, the silence had softened. There was still no TV. She didn't like the noise. But there was always music now—Carnatic flute in the mornings, soft jazz in the evenings, and sometimes lullabies while she cooked.

She started bringing lunch to work in a tiffin-box. Always simple. Always warm. The middle compartment, always empty.

A quiet gesture. A private promise.

And every Friday, she walked past Rue des Jasmins. Not to search. Not to wait.

Just to remember.

The old temple had become a daycare, its outer walls freshly painted. The scent of sandalwood still clung faintly to the stone. Sometimes, she imagined Meena there— sweeping, laughing, cooking too much rice.

She didn't need every answer. Some stories remained complete, even with missing pages. What mattered, in the end, was what she chose to carry.

ONE EVENING, as the sun slipped behind the rooftops, she sat by the window with a bowl of *dal* in her lap. She opened the tiffin-box just slightly. Not to read the letters again. Just enough to let the scent of sandalwood rise into the room.

Then she closed it, set it gently back on the shelf—between the tin and the ticket.

Three objects.

Like sisters.

She didn't cry.

She didn't need to.

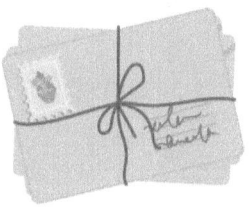

The Postman Always Delivers...Eventually

Flora McGowan

WHEN EMILE O'NEILL needed to earn extra money for Christmas, Millie, his grandmother, suggested he apply for work as a temporary postman. He could deliver the mail early in the morning before his college classes began. Emile wasn't as enthusiastic about the idea as Millie thought he might be, being a young man who found he needed his sleep (beauty not entering into the equation, being tall and lanky. His growth spurts had always been upwards without any corresponding increase in girth). Maybe not a full eight hours but rising at 6 a.m. (or possibly earlier) did not fill him with quite as much fervour. His keenness waned even further when, after passing the aptitude test, he was informed of his route.

"Of course, being a temp, I've drawn the short straw with the dross round. All the hilly streets, houses with ferocious dogs...and Hobb's Way!"

He looked so forlorn that Millie experienced a momentary pang of regret that she'd suggested he apply for the job to ease his cash flow problems but quickly pushed it to one side. She had blue eyes which, at this moment, looked anxiously across at her grandson. "I'm sure you'll cope admirably," she said, resisting the urge to cross her fingers behind her back as she spoke.

"At least I don't have to wear shorts," Emile said, gazing down ruefully at his knobbly knees atop thin shanks. "Not unless I want to, that is." He and his grandmother exchanged grins as they acknowledged this unlikely scenario. "Just sturdy footwear."

***

AS EMILE prepared to go out on his first round, Jack, an older postman who was also packing his own bag before heading out, tapped Emile's arm to gain his attention and said:

"You'll be fine, lad. A big strapping fella like you should manage the route easy." He cast a wary glance around the sorting office to see who might be listening in to their conversation. Emile looked as well.

"Don't you mind anything you hear about Hobb's Way," the man continued. "It's all just talk, rumour, local legend. You know how these things start. When my kids were small they used to play around the old house, you'll figure the one. Used to dare each other to knock on the door and run away. Told themselves ghost stories to frighten each other." He chuckled at the memory. "There's nothing to it. They're all grown up now with kids of their own. No trouble ever came to them there."

"So why all these signs, then?" Emile nodded his head

towards the section where his post was sorted. For Hobb's Way, there were various notices detailing that householders preferred to come into the depot and collect their mail themselves.

"Ah, now. That'll be because of all the fuss there was a few years back. Lemme see." Jack tipped his head back and screwed up his eyes for a moment, deep in concentration. "There was trouble with a chap, must be five, maybe more years ago. If you mind, Hobb's Way is the end of the route. Frank, that was his name. Nice lad, really. Not much older than you. Was allergic to bees. Or possibly wasps. Got stung once walking through Chapman Gardens and his leg swelled up twice the size. He'd not been in the job long." Jack looked over his shoulder to check the supervisor wasn't around and then hitched his buttocks onto the edge of the sorting counter before continuing his tale.

"Anyhow, one day he simply disappeared," Jack said. "Never even finished his round. Got as far as Chancer's Lane and that was it. Gone. The folk from Hobb's Way came and complained they never got their post, and since then, most of them come and collect it from here. Frank was never seen again. He'd done a runner. Not sure what was in his bag that day but whatever it was, he took it with him. Rumour was it could have been a big footie betting win or a cheque, something like that. Strange. He didn't seem the sort."

With a sigh Jack moved away from the desk and, grabbing his mailbag, slipped the strap over his head. Settling it into position so that the sack rested on his hip, he added, "Always thought he was a nice lad."

The first week presented no problems to Emile. The

weather was mild for November, but still he decided shorts were not an option. No large, ferocious snarling dogs blocked his path or chased him down the road, and happily, as Jack had foreseen, there were no letters to deliver to Hobb's Way. However, he still had to walk down that road with it being the direct route back to the depot to drop off his empty mailbag, as he had classes to get to. He was aware other posties usually doubled back up Chancer's Lane, taking the longer 'scenic route' instead.

He moved swiftly down Hobb's Way, casting quick glances left and right, trying to decide which was the haunted house from Jack's tale. However, several of the places looked like candidates, with high walls and tall leafy trees with overhanging branches that tapped him on the shoulder as he passed. He saw few people about and those he encountered looked at him as warily as he regarded his surroundings.

His fortunes, however, turned in the second week, a dreary seven days of constant rain, culminating in hailstones the size and consistency of marbles, and a thunderstorm with lightning flashes that could illuminate the depths of the earth. Which was where Emile felt he might be headed as, unhappily, there was a letter addressed to 'End House, Hobb's Way.' There was no recipient name or street number given. Furthermore, during his reluctant trek down Hobb's Way, he had to stop at each house to ascertain its name, peering through the heavy rain that dripped from the brim of his hat onto his auburn eyebrows before running in rivulets down the side of his face. His eyes eventually alighted on an old weatherbeaten wooden sign declaring it to be 'End House.' With a sigh, he pulled his jacket collar up higher and turned towards the building.

Opening the rusted creaking gate, which resisted his first attempt to move it, he thought, *it doesn't feel like anyone has opened this gate in a while*. He trudged up the gravel path, overgrown with tufts of grass and rambling weeds. Persistent rain added to the natural gloom and made it hard to distinguish any features. The house appeared as a dark, shadowy feature amidst densely wooded grounds. His spirits sank yet further as he could locate no letterbox in the front door, nor any postal box attached to the wall or on a post near to the building.

He pushed the bell but heard no sound coming from within. Deciding the bell was not connected he knocked, waited, then knocked again. The door was a surprisingly snug fit with no gaps at either side or underneath through which he could slip the missive. Time was passing and he wanted to complete his deliveries and return to the depot so he could dry out.

He peered through the nearest window but it was covered in dirt and grime, and he could make nothing out. He thought about rapping on the glass but considered the surrounding wood looked too rotten and fragile to withstand rough treatment. The last thing he wanted was a repair bill eating into his wages.

Despondently, he gazed at the envelope in his hand, considering what to do. The writing was an elegant copperplate, written possibly by a hand using a fountain pen—his mind went into flights of fancy inspired by the old gothic house, and for a second, he imagined a quill. The envelope itself was thick, cream in colour, and screamed expensive. There was no return address. As he contemplated the item in his hand, a large plop of rain landed plum on the word 'Hobb's,' the resultant splash creating, for a second, 'Hobson.' Emile rubbed his eyes, looked again but merely saw an indecipherable brown splodge.

Stashing the letter once more in his bag, he retraced his steps back down the stony path to the street. As luck would have it—at last! He spied someone in the process of slipping through the gate next door.

"I say!" Emile called out. "Excuse me. You don't happen to know your neighbour?"

Dark beady eyes looked him up and down from the shelter of an encompassing anorak hood. The head gave a little shake, causing water droplets to fly in all directions. Emile took a step back, despite the fact that he was already soaked to the skin and a little more liquid would make no difference.

"Nope, no neighbours. No one lives there." The man turned to go, then seeing Emile open his mouth as if to protest, added, "House has been emptied these last twenty years or more." And with that, he sped up the path and was out of sight before Emile could question him further.

EMILE OFTEN POPPED round to visit his grandmother in the evening to check that she was well, with the added bonus that she'd usually feed him. "So who," he asked, as he dried the dishes after their meal while she washed, "would send a letter to an empty house where no one has lived for years, with no letterbox to receive any post?"

After placing the final saucepan on the draining rack, Millie removed her washing up gloves. She stood tall for a second, stretching her back after being hunched over the sink. "What did you do with the letter?" she asked.

"I thought about leaving it under the mat," Emile said, then seeing Millie's disapproving frown, added, "but that seemed the easy way out. When I took this job on, I guaranteed to deliver the mail to the best of my abilities, and leaving a letter under the mat did not seem secure or right." Millie nodded. "Plus, the mat was old and tatty and wouldn't have hidden so much as the stamp in the corner. Besides, I know this is only a temp job, but I might find myself in need of extra cash next Christmas, or during the summer, so I really want to do the job properly. Not cut any corners. Just in case." He paused, then added. "I know most of the residents come to the depot once a week unless they're expecting something important, but there's no notice to say the householder of 'End House' prefers to collect his or her mail. So, I thought I'd better try and deliver it. I don't want any complaints."

Millie smiled and nodded her understanding and agreement with his sentiments to do the job properly, plus his possible future requirements for extra money. However, inside she was feeling perturbed. When Emile had mentioned Hobb's Way as being part of his route, it brought back memories of an old black and white film. She couldn't remember the details. It had been a science fiction film about Martians or aliens. She recalled some ghosts haunting an old building and that 'Hobs' was an old English name for the devil. She'd shivered involuntarily when he'd mentioned he thought the letter was addressed to 'Hobson' which, in her mind, implied the son of the devil, and she hoped that wasn't some sort of prophecy or warning. Not that she'd heard anything about Hobb's Way, but it was always, she had found, best to be prepared. One never knew what might be around the next corner.

She glanced across at her grandson as he hung the tea towel on the rail to dry. He was normally a cheerful young man, unfazed by the problems of life. As someone who had grown up with red hair and a smattering of freckles across his nose, he was usually ready to face the world head on. However, recently the smiles that normally graced his visage were absent, and his brows could be seen drawn into an almost perpetual frown as he considered various problems, the most pressing at present being rising rent, unwelcome at any time but more so at the start of the festive season. And now, when he had made positive steps to improve his cash flow, he was given a postal route littered with problems. Specifically, a road that most people tended to avoid in daylight, and a letter proving impossible to deliver.

HOWEVER, the next day, Emile had a second letter to deliver to the house, again addressed in the same copperplate handwriting, and also the following day, until by the end of the week he had five undelivered letters in a cubby hole at the depot. He'd resorted to sticking a slip of paper to the front door detailing where the householder could collect their post.

"I feel it's a test of some sort," Emile grumbled. "Like an initiation from the powers that be, or a hazing from the regular posties who object to temps—although I've relieved someone from the horrors of the Hobb's Way round."

"Yes, it could be a test," Millie agreed. "But maybe not one set specifically for you."

If Emile didn't like the idea of undelivered letters, he

liked the thought of someone besting him in some silly test or prank even less, and so, after much thought on the matter, he decided to venture down to the pub in Chancer's Lane. Maybe one or two of the locals who were out at work during the day when he was delivering his post would be able to shed some light on the situation.

Millie agreed. "It would do you good to get out a bit more," she told him. "All work and no play et cetera."

Emile grinned. She was worse than his mother when urging him to do something. Therefore, after eating dinner, he duly strolled down to The Chancer's Arms. He resolved to limit himself to one drink in view of his cash flow crisis, maybe half a pint, just something so that he had a drink in his hands when he questioned people.

However, on entering the premises, it felt like he'd arrived on the wrong night. The place was empty. Was there football on the telly or something he'd forgotten about? While he lamented a possible wrong decision, the barman was clearly delighted to see him. He instantly picked up a towel and gave the bar a vigorous rubdown, as if to indicate he'd been very busy and Emile had just missed the early evening rush.

Wanting to play it casually after his first frantic look around, Emile sauntered across to the bar. He gave what he hoped was a suitable smile, while patting his pockets to ensure he had his student ID in case he was asked.

The barman wiped his hands on the towel, placed it to one side and, raising an eyebrow as if to indicate Emile was next in some imaginary queue, asked, "What'll it be, squire?"

For a second, Emile's mind went blank. He wasn't much of a drinker; however, he knew regular barflies drank beer

from the pumps. "Umm...I'll have a pint of...IPA please,"
he said, naming the cheapest option.

Soon his pint was on the counter. The barman hovered.
As Emile had already eaten, he didn't want to ask for crisps
or nuts but felt he ought to say something. He took a tenta-
tive sip and decided the beer wasn't too strong, while his
mind furiously went round in circles searching for a suitable
opening. However, the gods were smiling on him as the
barman himself, keen to encourage someone who might
develop into a regular drinker in his establishment, uttered
the perfect question.

"New to this area, are you? Don't think we've had the
pleasure before."

"Actually," Emile replied, quickly wiping the back of his
hand across his mouth. "I'm the new postman." He smiled,
hoping the barman wouldn't guess that it was merely
temporary seasonal work.

"Ahh. That's interesting. Not sure we've had the local
postie in here before. There again, not sure I've seen a local
postie full stop."

"Yes, I gather some people prefer to collect their own
mail." Emile paused. "But I'm here now if people don't
want the trek up to the sorting office in the rain. Or snow."
He hoped he wasn't laying it on too thick.

The barman introduced himself as Mike and, picking
up a fresh towel, began polishing beer glasses. "Seem to
recall there was something about the local postman some
years back. What was it now?" He opened a door behind
him and called out, "Dad! Dad, will you come here a
minute?" After a short wait, an elderly gentleman shuffled
into view. Mike indicated Emile, who relayed the story Jack

had told him about the previous postman disappearing with the mail.

"That's right," agreed Mike's dad. He chuckled. "We started a betting pool. People came up with all sorts of silly reasons as to how and why he'd gone, how long it would be before he was found. That sort of thing. Of course, folk were angry, but it helped to calm the inflamed tempers to make a joke of it."

Emile murmured agreement. "What sort of reasons?" he asked, with what he hoped was an encouraging smile. He sipped his beer and waited.

Mike also stared intently at his father, and the older man, relishing the attention, scratched his head, pursed his lips and kept his audience of two waiting while he thought.

"He'd gone through a time portal. *Picnic at Hanging Rock* had been on the telly, so that was a popular one. Taken by spacemen for experiments, or an intergalactic zoo. Someone suggested the white slave trade—didn't know they took men, thought it was all young women—no accounting for taste, I suppose. Or ran off with a girlfriend..." he shrugged "...or boyfriend. Kidnapped by fairies, or pixies, leprechauns—something about a pot of gold at the end of a rainbow, as it always seems to rain down Hobb's Way!" He let out another chortle. "Or goblins. In fact, a witness said he saw Frank talking to a strange little man, but he'd just come out of the Red Lion pub—the witness, not the strange man—so that story was taken with a pinch of salt." He leaned forward, beckoning to Emile as if what he'd said was a secret. "They water the beer there."

He cleared his throat, straightened up and continued with the suggestions people had laid bets on. "But spirited away somehow. Me, I thought if he'd taken all that money, travel for sure, next plane to South America. Or Spain."

Emile found it hard to keep the smile from his face. He couldn't wait to pass this gossip onto his grandmother.

EMILE RESISTED his grandmother's pleas to bring a letter home with him so she could examine it. In the end, he agreed to her suggestion that she tag along on his delivery, joining him at the junction of Hobb's Way and Chancer's Lane. Once again, Emile had a letter addressed to 'End House.' Immediately upon reaching their destination Millie noted something odd.

"You didn't tell me that 'End House' is not, in fact, the house at the end of the street," she complained.

Emile stared first at his grandmother, then at the letter in his hand before shifting his gaze to the house in question, as if it had been rearranged in the street overnight. He opened his mouth, closed it and then asked, "Does it matter?"

"Hmm, possibly not. Just curious," she replied. "The end of what, I wonder?" She opened the creaking gate with a little push and made her way up the path.

"And the house is boarded up. That's why there's no letterbox in the door. The door's behind this hardboard." She gave it a firm tat-tat with her knuckles. Noting Emile's crestfallen expression, she said, "I expect it was dark and wet, and you were flustered having to deliver a letter to this —" she waved an arm around to encompass the overgrown shrubbery bordering the path, the ramshackle house and generally neglected grounds, "—place."

Millie asked to see the envelope. She lifted it close to eye level and peered at it. She held it up to the light—for once, there was pale, watery sunlight filtering down through the trees—and then picked unsuccessfully at the edges of the stamp.

"As you say, it's a good quality envelope, thick, so I cannot see if there is actually anything inside or not. Remember, in the early days of postal delivery, letters were paid on receipt and not on posting. People refused to pay if they received a blank piece of paper. So, soldiers in particular made a habit of sending blank letters to their wives which indicated they were safe and well. Or alive, at any rate."

She pointed to the stamp. "Nor did you say it was posted first class. Why use expensive methods when there is a cheaper second class option, and as far as we can tell, no one at home to receive the letter anyway?" She paused. "In the films there would be a rare, valuable penny black stamp hidden underneath this stamp, or a sliver of microfilm, or something." She giggled.

But whatever comment she thought of adding was forgotten as Emile cried, "What's that?" and, pointing to some greenery, the fronds of which were waving despite there being no breeze, he loped up the path that meandered around the side of the house. Millie scurried after him, unable to keep pace with his longer stride. When she caught up with him, Emile had stopped in a small clearing, next to a decrepit garden house. Millie took a second to catch her breath. Facing them was a strange man. He was short, about five feet tall, and stout. He had an oval face and a completely bald head. His hands were a labyrinth of wrinkles but his beady eyes were bright and clear.

"I knew you'd come!" he exclaimed, hopping up and down in delight. "Knew it. Knew it." His wizened face split into a huge grin and he clapped his hands together.

"And you would be...?" Millie asked.

"Me?" His brows drew together. "Me? I'm not important." His face relaxed and the frown instantly disappeared. "I knew you'd come back if I wrote."

"You wrote the letters!" Emile cried. "Why? If you live here, why write to yourself?"

"I wrote because I wanted somebody to come. And you have. It worked. Finally, it worked." The little old man hugged himself.

"Tell me, how long have you been writing?" Millie asked.

"Oh, for ages. A long time. All the other postmen came maybe once but they never returned. But you did. I just knew you would." He skipped about. "I said I'd get help and now finally you've arrived."

"Help?" Millie and Emile said, almost in unison.

"For Frank." Then, as if suddenly remembering the reason for summoning help, he beckoned for Millie and Emile to follow him. He picked his way through the overgrown weeds to the garden house. The wooden door hung drunkenly on its hinges. He disappeared inside.

Millie shared a look with Emile. She had a momentary thought that the man had disappeared into a time portal or another dimension until she heard the scuffling sounds of movement coming from within. Carefully she stepped over the threshold, Emile close behind her. A musty smell of mould and mildew assailing her nostrils didn't bode well.

When her eyes grew accustomed to the gloom, she gazed around. It was a hexagonal structure with scattered remnants of chairs and cushions. The panes of glass in the windows were cracked and broken. Dust specks danced in the air and thick cobwebs descended from the ceiling.

Slumped on a two-seater in an alcove, she saw Frank. Or what had once been Frank. A cap was perched on his skull at a jaunty angle. Clothes hung in tatters from bony shoulders. The cloth covering his legs ended at his knee joints. One disarticulated leg bone lay on the grimy floor.

"Shorts?" Emile whispered. "A schoolboy?"

Millie shook her head. "Look." Emile's gaze followed to where she pointed. He could just make out on the ground what appeared to be a bag or satchel. He moved forward and tentatively lifted the flap. All that remained inside was a pile of mouldering paper.

"Didn't you think to call for an ambulance? Get a doctor if Frank was ill?" Millie asked the little man.

The man frowned and shook his head. "Ambulance? Doctor? What good would they be? They cannot deliver the post!"

"Ah well," Millie sighed. "I think we know what happened to Hobb's Way's last regular postman. Becoming unwell, he came inside to rest. Our reclusive friend here volunteered to get help. Unfortunately, he seems to be one of life's innocents, and his 'help' consisted of writing letters to attract another mail carrier. However, with the house boarded up and the road's reputation, it's been rather a long time before one appeared."

"How do you think he died?" Emile asked. "If it is Frank, Jack told me he was a young chap about my age. You have to be reasonably fit to be a postal worker, so it can't have been his heart or anything like that. Dog bite, perhaps?"

"Something similar, I would say. Didn't this Jack mention he was allergic to wasp or bee stings? Often these have a cumulative effect. The first sting would have made him ill; a subsequent sting may have been fatal. Poor lad. Managed to get to this garden house to wait for help, and all this person..." Millie gestured towards the man who was hovering over the remnants of the postbag, "...was concerned about was who was going to finish delivering the mail."

"Why didn't the police or someone find the body? They must have done a search when he went missing, especially as he still had the post with him."

"Presumably because they were looking for a man, someone alive, who they thought had done a runner, possibly with something of value. I dare say there were house-to-house enquiries. But what would the authorities have made of this place?" Millie sighed. "Some police constable would have knocked on the door and, finding no answer and the house boarded up, moved on to the next house. They were, after all, looking for a person, not a corpse. They had no reason to check the grounds."

"But the smell? A decomposing body stinks, surely!"

"A decomposing body in a garden hut behind the main house, which may then have had its door and windows intact, made it unlikely for any stench to be transmitted on the wind," Millie shrugged. "After a month or two of advanced decomposition, thanks to flies, beetles, rats and what have you, the soft tissue would be largely gone. Blood and other bodily fluids dried up and evaporated."

"Okay. So what about all the previous letters our friend here sent?" Emile gestured to the man.

"I suspect you'll find them back at the depot. After all,

the residents of this road like to collect their post and so a stash addressed to 'End House' wouldn't look out of place, especially if it was thought the house was empty. With no return address, they may be in some sort of cellar or archive, and I dare say a few merely got thrown away. Plus, I suspect our friend wrote sporadically, whenever he noticed a new postal worker on the block, which you may remember, is not very often as the postmen before you tended to avoid this road if possible. It wasn't until you came along and the man saw you walking this part of your route that he started writing once more."

"But I still don't see why he used expensive paper, or envelopes at least, and first class stamps. Why not simply stop me on my rounds or phone someone or knock on a door? Why the letters?"

"The poor man seems to me to be suffering from something like savant syndrome, where a person has a special ability but may be lacking in other social, intellectual, or emotional skills," Millie said. "Think of those people who can play a song after hearing it once, or paint a scene in minute detail. This chap has artistic abilities."

"Not a goblin then," Emile said.

"No, nor a leprechaun or elf living at the bottom of the garden." Millie paused before adding, "Simply an artistic man with beautiful writing, and a fixation on postal workers. Similar to small boys who rush out to greet their postal worker or garbageman. One woman I worked with had a young son who persistently phoned the police after being shown in preschool what to do in an emergency. It made his day to be given a ride in a police car—but only after he promised not to phone again unless it was urgent. Yes, in some ways I think our friend here retains much of the innocence of childhood. But beautiful writing. I can imagine him as a monk in a medieval monastery illustrating all those lovely gospels!"

Millie turned to leave. "Come along Emile, we'd best call the authorities to deal with this and inform the poor lad's parents. What must they have thought all these years? Their son accused of flight and theft!" She paused, and with a small smile added, "I wonder if anyone in the pub placed a bet on 'with a bee, in the garden house?' "

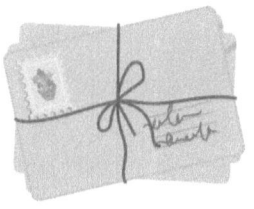

Lab's Labours Lost

Melissa Behrend

"WHAT THE DEVIL?" Evelyn turned the envelope over and stared, nonplused. She stood at her desk, as if in a trance.

"What is it?" Mary's eyes widened as she watched her friend. Evelyn was rarely at a loss for words, so this was noteworthy. Mary rose from the couch and walked from the living room to where Evelyn stood. The envelope in her hand was unremarkable. "Evelyn?"

The piece of correspondence had fallen from behind a picture frame when Evelyn did a little unplanned redecorating. Well, what she'd actually done was hip check the desk and sent everything toppling. Evelyn tore her eyes from the missive and turned to Mary. She showed her friend the front of the envelope, where the name '*Evelyn*' was written in shaky cursive. "This is John's handwriting."

Mary's hand went to her throat. "I wonder when he hid it there?"

Evelyn shrugged. "I don't know. Maybe he meant for this to be some sort of…present for me? A silly little scavenger hunt or something? He used to love to leave clues around on my birthday or our anniversary. Oh, and on Halloween. His right brain loved a puzzle." She sank down into the desk chair, still clutching the letter, unopened. She made no move to open it.

Mary placed a hand on her shoulder. "Aren't you going to read it?"

Evelyn held the envelope out in front of her and stared at it, as if the idea were foreign. "I'm a bit afraid, if you want to know the truth."

Mary tsked. "Afraid? You? You've never been afraid a day in your life. Now, open the letter." This drew a smile from Evelyn.

"You flatter me. But you're right. Okay, here goes—" But instead of opening the envelope, she placed it flat on the desk and slid it to the middle of her blotter. Then she stared at it as if it might bite.

Mary reached out and placed a hand on her shoulder. "Would you like to be alone? I can go."

Evelyn looked up and smiled; she dismissed the idea with a wave of her hand. "No, no. Please stay." Mary gave her space, though. She retreated to the living room and perched on the edge of a recliner, clutching a pillow to her midsection.

Tea first, then the letter. She popped out of the chair and went to the kitchen. Filled her electric kettle. Waited. Opened a cabinet. Calming tea? Chamomile would do. Dropped it in the pot, added hot water. Evelyn didn't procrastinate. But she did now. Brought the pot through to her desk, filled her teacup. Sat. Stood.

"Ready?"

Mary's voice caused her to jump. Evelyn's hand went to her chest. "Mary! I'd forgotten you were there."

"Sorry. I should go." Mary half rose, but Evelyn waved her back into her seat.

"No, no. I just...this is a lot. I've not heard John's voice in a year. You think you're, well, not over it, but you think you've dealt with the pain, and then..." Her voice swelled with emotion. A tear formed at the corner of her eye; she wiped it away. She carefully unsealed the envelope and slid a single sheet of notepaper out. Of course he would be brief. As she read, John's rough voice narrated. A smile touched her lips. Then it died. Her brow furrowed. Evelyn dropped the hand holding the letter to her side, the other went to her chest. Her blood ran cold.

Mary rushed to her friend's side; squeezed her hand. "What is it? What'd he say?"

For a moment, Evelyn couldn't answer. "He said he was in danger and he feared for his safety..." She trailed off.

Mary tilted her head. Waited.

Evelyn sank into the desk chair, ran a hand through her short, steel gray hair. "This letter is dated just days before John's death. They told me it was natural causes. But if what John says is right, maybe it wasn't a heart attack."

Mary inhaled sharply. "What was John worried about?"

Evelyn barked out a laugh. Looked off into space. When she turned back to Mary, her expression was bewildered. "The letter's vague; said he couldn't spell it out because he didn't want to endanger me." She waved the note around and laughed again, the sound unhinged. "But he does say if he turns up dead, then it was murder."

Mary's face scrunched. "Murder?"

"Yes."

"Maybe you should start from the beginning."

Evelyn stood and nodded to the kitchen. "Let's get something stronger than tea."

Mary placed her mug down on the table with a definitive thunk. She gathered the crumbs in front of her and brushed them off the table into her palm. She stood and walked to Evelyn's trash can, talking over her shoulder. "Well, now what? Are you going to call the sheriff?"

Evelyn harrumphed. "And what would he do?"

Mary faced her friend, put a hand on her hip. "Well, you're the widow. You can have his body exhumed. Once you prove it's murder…"

Evelyn shook her head. "I'm not sure. Let me think on it. I need to do some research—"

"Investigate on your own, you mean?" When Evelyn hesitated, Mary walked back to the kitchen table, retook her seat. She placed a hand on her friend's wrist. "I'll help you. Whatever you need."

Evelyn smiled. "Thank you. I'll let you know."

Evelyn spent the rest of the day in John's office, combing through his old files, reading documents, and googling. She found quite a few interesting things, but none seemed to have anything to do with what she wanted to know. She even stumbled upon a file folder of old emails, but she couldn't make heads nor tails of them. They appeared to be between John and the administrative assistants of a couple of pharmaceutical companies. "Why did you save these, dear?" she muttered aloud, wishing he could answer.

She settled into John's huge old leather chair and picked up her phone. "Indira? Hello, it's Evelyn." Uncapping her pen and turning to a fresh page in her notebook, she started to question her old friend. "Yes, well, I'm hoping you can help me with something…" She paused to listen.

"It's probably nothing, but do you remember what sort of grants John worked on before he retired?" She scribbled in her notebook as Indira tried to recall. "I know, it was a while ago…" Evelyn's pen stopped. "Oh, he did? I didn't realize. Would you have time to meet with me sometime this week? I'd love to come in and take a look at anything he might have had a hand in—" Evelyn's face took on a pensive look. Uncertain how much to share, she replied, "It'll sound silly, I know, but I came across some scribbles of his and I thought it might have something to do with his work there. Maybe if I bring it in, you and I might be able to match it to a grant? Guess I'm missing him lately." Decided to play the sorrowful widow card and it worked.

"Oh, thank you so much, Indira. I'll see you then." She ended the call and tapped her pen against her lips.

———————

"KNOCK, KNOCK!" Mary's chipper voice called as she let herself, and a cold December wind, in. Evelyn followed her nose, and Mary's voice, to the foyer. She beamed at her prompt friend and eyed the white bakery box in her hands. They had a standing coffee date every morning, but Mary rarely showed up with more than her charming personality.

"What's that lovely smell?"

Mary held up the goodies. "I brought croissants from All You Knead is Love." Evelyn took the box so Mary could shuck her coat and shoes.

"You braved the elements for pastries? I'd say you shouldn't have…but instead, I'll simply say thank you." She brought the box closer to her nose and inhaled. "Still warm."

"Hard to believe in this weather." Mary hung her coat on a hook and added her stocking cap. "I figured you burned the midnight oil and might need a little boost this morning. Smells like you've already got the caffeine percolating."

Evelyn laughed. "Right on both counts. Come on through. You look like you could use a little warming up." Mary shivered and agreed.

They slipped into chairs at Evelyn's dining room table, where, despite the cold, a bar of sunshine fell on the coffee mugs and croissants in front of them. Once settled, Evelyn began to regale her friend with the prior day's search history.

"Were you able to find out what John had been working on?"

Evelyn held her hand out and tilted it from side to side. "Sort of. Once I hit a dead end in John's office, I called Indira, his colleague at the lab."

"Did she actually remember what he'd been working on? He retired quite a while ago..." Mary rose to get a refill. She offered the pot to Evelyn, who shook her head.

"She did. She gave me a list. But she reminded me of something else..."

Mary made her way back to the table. "What's that?"

"Well, you know John," Evelyn rolled her eyes as she chewed. "He liked to keep busy. Once he 'retired' he was always searching for something to do. Took up a million hobbies—"

Mary sat back down, her coffee mug hitting the table a

little too hard, a couple of drops bouncing out onto the table. "Oh! The kites!"

Evelyn sputtered, remembering. "The kites. And the photography. And the jigsaw puzzles, and the garden, and the birdwatching, and the…" She motioned with her hand. "Well, once he got bored of all that, he decided to go back to the lab to see if he could be of any help. See if there was anything he could get into there." She buttered another section of croissant, then put it back down on her plate.

Mary peeled a croissant apart and narrowed her eyes. "Why do I get the feeling he found something to get into?"

Evelyn pointed her butter knife at her. "Give the lady a Kewpie doll. He sure did. Indira said the university partnered with a non-profit upstate to do some research on a cancer drug, specifically for pediatric cancer. Indira said she and Scott were happy to have him assist, put his excellent grant writing skills to good use." Evelyn popped the pastry into her mouth. "She also said he helped write up a grant for a clinical trial, something to do with migraines."

Mary sighed. "Wish I'd known about that one. I'd have let them experiment on me." She paused and glanced down at the table. "And what did Indira have to say about all this?" She gestured to the letter and the notepad next to Evelyn's left hand.

"Well, I didn't give her any details but I did set up a meeting with her. I asked to see the documents he'd drafted." She shrugged. "I didn't want to give anything away. After all, John didn't say who he was afraid of…"

Mary gasped. "You don't think—?"

"I don't know what to think. But maybe I will after I visit with her."

SNOW ACCOMPANIED Evelyn into the lobby of the university's science building. The young man at the desk was unknown to her, but it had been years since she'd stepped foot inside. She gave him a small wave and a big smile as she approached. "Hello there!"

"Good afternoon, ma'am. How can I help you today?" The skinny, bespectacled student beamed at her, ready to help. His name tag read 'Nathan Stone.'

Evelyn placed her clasped hands on the counter. "Well, Nathan, I'm here to meet with Dr. Indira Grant. I have a one o'clock appointment. Evelyn White."

Nathan nodded. "One moment. I'll call Dr. Grant for you." While Nathan was on the phone, Evelyn glanced around the lobby. Not much had changed; it rarely did in academia. What money there was in the budget went to more important things like equipment or textbooks (did they still use textbooks, she wondered, or was everything on computers these days?) The only noticeable changes were in the promotional materials. While academics had to publish or perish, in the scientific world, it often came down to research grants. Finding something new to show the world. John's specialty had been medical research, and he'd often been the one writing up grant proposals or analyzing data from experiments. The posters around her now promoted a new lecture series on DNA analysis and whole genome sequencing. While she didn't understand it, she knew John would have been over the moon about it. She missed him.

"She'll be right up."

Evelyn turned back to Nathan. "Thank you so much."

She wandered over towards the far hallway where the scientists' labs were situated. Not a minute later, Indira appeared, her arms open for a hug.

"Evelyn! So good to see you. I've missed you. Come." The tiny woman turned and hustled down the hall, not waiting to see if Evelyn followed. Evelyn laughed to herself. Who wouldn't listen to this woman? She felt sorry for any student in Indira's class who dared to forget an assignment or clean up their station.

"I hope you don't mind chatting in the lab?" Indira called back over her shoulder. "Grades are due."

Evelyn chuckled. "Say no more." Gradebooks still haunted her dreams; she often woke up in a sweat, worried she'd forgotten to submit them. Their heels click-clacked along the shiny, black tiled floors. Once they were seated on stools, Evelyn spun to watch Indira poke and prod at something in a petri dish. Her friend frowned. Evelyn wasn't sure if she was disappointed or focused. Whatever it was, she finally shook her head, made a note on her pad and sat up, giving Evelyn her full attention.

"So, you said you had some questions? Your phone call was a bit mysterious. I haven't seen you since…" Indira's face fell. She opened her mouth to apologize but Evelyn stopped her.

"Oh, no. It's fine. But like I said, I'm just curious about what John was working on." Evelyn glanced around the lab, searching for other ears. The only ones she saw belonged to the skeleton hanging on the wall behind her. Someone, a student she assumed, had given the poor thing Mardi Gras beads and a handbag. He, or she, stood out in the otherwise sterile space, where everything shined. Nothing out of place. Indira noticed where her eyes had gone.

"Ah, yes. Poor Skelly. The students can't help them-selves. They dress him up, I undress him...it's a vicious cycle. John loved to encourage them. I'm pretty sure he started it, actually." The two women laughed.

Evelyn nodded. "Sounds right. You know, he'd come to my classroom at Halloween and decorate, setting up elabo-rate dioramas and life-sized figures to give my third graders a thrill." The two ruminated on it for a moment, smiles on their faces.

"Do you miss it?" Indira asked. "Teaching, I mean?"

Evelyn shook head vehemently. "Not a bit." Evelyn smiled. "Actually, that's part of why I'm here."

"Halloween? Did you want to borrow Skelly?" Her voice was serious, but she smiled to let Evelyn know she was kidding.

Evelyn batted away the idea. "No, no. You see, I knocked over a picture frame a few days ago and out fell a letter from John—"

Indira gasped. Evelyn nodded. She agreed, it was gasp-worthy. "At first, I thought perhaps he'd done some sort of scavenger hunt before he died and forgot about it..." She glanced around the lab again to make sure no one else had entered. "But then I read the letter."

Indira was enraptured. She'd leaned forward so far on her stool, Evelyn feared she'd fall on the hard tiles. At least they were clean. "What did it say? Are these the 'scribbles' you said you found?"

"Well, yes and no. Remember when I asked you about the last grants John worked on?"

"Yes, of course." Indira's tone was clipped. Evelyn real-ized it had only been a few days since their phone call.

"Well, John's letter was written days before his death.

He said if anything were to happen to him, to look at the grants."

Indira inhaled sharply. Her hand flew to her mouth. "No. I thought he died of a heart attack."

"So did I. But a heart attack can be caused by a lot of different things. I cross-referenced the grants you told me about with whatever I could find online about those studies—"

Indira held up a hand. "What do you mean? Why would you look at those? We don't do anything here worth murdering someone over." She gave a firm shake of her head and glanced down at the table, avoiding Evelyn's eyes. "I think John was mistaken. We both know he was getting on in years. I mean, he'd retired—"

Evelyn's dander was up. "Are you going to sit there and tell me you think John was losing it? Both you and Scott welcomed him back with open arms. Why would you do that if he were slipping even a little?"

Indira's mouth opened and closed like a fish. She glanced back up, her cheeks colouring. "I...No. You're right. I'm sorry. He wasn't. I just don't understand what you're saying. We don't do any work that gets our names in the papers, we don't do any work that brings in the big bucks—"

"Ah," Evelyn said with a cheeky grin. "There's where you're wrong."

"What do you mean?"

Evelyn slid her tablet out of her handbag and powered it on. "There's this one." Then she opened another tab. "And this one..." By the time they'd read through everything Evelyn had found, the situation was both clearer and muddier.

"Huh. Well, I must admit, I did not know about these... developments." Indira pushed back from the table. "Maybe we should go through to my office? I have some of the supporting documentation there. We can take a look, but I can't imagine we'll find anything. Scott will have some of it as well, because one of those grants was his baby."

Evelyn stood and followed, but she gave Skelly a back-wards glance. She didn't trust him.

"I THINK that's the last of them," Indira slid a file folder over to her. Evelyn added it to the pile on her corner of the mahogany desk. Indira's lab was pristine and sterile, but her office was the exact opposite. Evelyn had no idea how the woman found anything. It was a miracle she knew where these files were. Indira hit a few keys on her computer and pulled up a screen. "I have several documents here related to those studies; I'll tackle these."

Without looking up, Evelyn muttered, "This migraine trial, it was commissioned by—"

"Oh, no! We're not even supposed to say their name aloud." She laughed at Evelyn's expression. "Kidding. But only just. All hush-hush. The makers of the drug really wanted it to be a blind study."

Evelyn's eyebrows rose higher than her hairline. "And did it work?" She shook her head. "The drug, I mean?"

Indira's face was non-committal. "Too soon to tell. This new drug could, potentially, be a lifesaver for migraineurs, but those days are far ahead of us. However, there have been some murmurings among the testers..." She turned back to her monitor and cocked her head as she read something there.

Evelyn leaned forward over the desk, trying to see what was onscreen. Indira had navigated to the stock exchange. "What is it?"

Indira sighed, her face troubled. "Well, I'm not sure… No, that can't be…"

Before she could finish, a brash middle-aged man burst through her office door. His brown hair was expensively coiffed, his lab coat open to model a Ralph Lauren polo and khakis. He pushed his Warby Parker glasses up on his nose as he glanced at Evelyn and then dismissed her as if he'd never seen her before. Although he had. Many times.

"Indira, I thought we had a meeting?" His arms flapped at his sides like an earthbound bird. Indira touched her forehead. "Ah, Scott. Sorry. I forgot. Evelyn and I—"

"You forgot?" He stepped over to Indira's desk and leaned his knuckles on it, scanning the files there. "What's all this?"

Ignoring his question, Indira motioned to Evelyn. "I believe you two know each other? You remember John's wife, Evelyn?"

Evelyn sat back in her chair and flashed a smile his way. "Hi, Scott. We met a few times, social functions here and there…"

Scott nodded and turned back to Indira. "So, what's going on?"

Indira minimized her screen and stood, pushing her chair back. Evelyn discreetly tidied the files in front of her. "Evelyn had some questions about the final grants John was working on—"

Scott's face flushed. "What? Why?" His eyes narrowed as he stared at Evelyn. "Is there a problem?"

Intrigued, Evelyn decided to poke the bear. She was the picture of calm, crossing one leg over the other. She opened a file and pretended to read. "Oh, no. Not at all. I recently found a letter John left me before he died. It was a bit cryptic. Made me want to learn more about what he'd been working on. Call it...idle curiosity."

Scott bit his lip, then huffed out a short breath. "Well, you know what they say about idle hands and curiosity..."

Evelyn tilted her head. "No, what do they say?"

Indira tutted. "I think you're mixing your metaphors, Scott."

He turned even redder than before. "Whatever. I believe that's all proprietary information, no business of yours. Besides," he glanced at Indira again, "we have a meeting." He turned on his heel and left the office. He tossed a scowl at Evelyn through the window.

"Wow, he's pleasant," Evelyn laughed. "Think I touched a nerve?"

Indira sighed. "He's very by-the-book. Having an outsider poke through our files is verboten, he's not wrong." She grabbed her tablet. "I do need to meet with him. Will you be okay on your own for half an hour?"

Evelyn nodded. "Of course. Thank you, again, for your help. I'll read through these, see if anything stands out."

Once Indira had gone, she opened her laptop to do a little cross-referencing. She decided to pay extra attention to anything with Scott's name on it.

EVELYN HAD SPENT the last thirty minutes reading everything she could about the cancer research grant and the migraine study. While Indira hadn't shared the name of the company behind the clinical trial, Evelyn had found it. And she'd quickly learned why Indira had been curious about the NYSE. The company's stock price had been on an uptake for months, mirroring the time of the trial. Someone could make a lot of money if they knew about it. But as she read, she realized it didn't make any sense, really. None of the participants were given the name of the drug or the manufacturer, and to bet on a possible 'cure' for migraines would be like purchasing a lottery ticket. There was no guarantee.

So, from there, she delved into the pediatric cancer study. She'd called Mary to verify and bounce some ideas off of her. The conversation had been short, but fruitful.

"Are you sure? Not the—?"

"Yes, the very same. Are you looking at it now?" She'd asked Mary to google the article so they could read through it at the same time.

"But this says those guys down in California, the tech bros or whatever they're called, developed it? I remember this was big news last year. Life-saving stuff." Mary read aloud as Evelyn scratched out some notes. Evelyn heard her gasp as she realized the repercussions. "Wait, so if what you're saying is true…?"

Evelyn nodded and then realized Mary couldn't see her. "Right. According to the file Indira handed me, it is, but in order to verify…" She shrugged to herself, her face sad. "I'll have to confront him. Seems like something you might kill for to keep quiet." Evelyn leaned back in her chair, tilted her head and looked at the ceiling. "But I can't prove it and I don't have a clue as to how to go about it." She sat quietly for a moment.

Mary tsked. "Oh, but you'll find a way. You always do. That's why John left you the note. He knew you'd read it and—" Mary stopped talking. "But Evelyn, be careful. If this man killed for it once, what's to say he won't do it again. Why don't you call the police before you confront him?"

However, Evelyn's chin had come back down and she was no longer listening to her friend. "You're right. You're exactly right."

"I am? Of course I am. You'll call the police?"

"What? Oh, not yet." Evelyn was up and headed for the door, their conversation largely forgotten.

———

"JOHN WAS RIGHT." Indira dropped her head into her hands and slumped back on her stool. "I can't believe it. How did I not see this?"

Evelyn reached across the table and patted her shoulder. "Well, it wasn't your project—" When she'd rushed from Indira's office, she'd met her friend in the hallway and pulled her into the lab. There, she'd shown her what she'd found online and in the grant documents.

"But I knew about the grant. We all did. It was ground-breaking. I don't know how I missed it." She looked up at Evelyn, tears in her eyes.

Evelyn pointed at her tablet. "For one, they changed the name…"

"How can you ever forgive me?" She jumped up and

took off before Evelyn could stop her. "I'm going to go and—"

"Wait!" Evelyn leapt to her feet and nearly tackled Indira at the door. "We can't just confront him!"

Indira stomped a foot. "We certainly can. I'll make him tell me exactly what he did—"

Evelyn sighed. "And you think he'll, what, admit to murder on top of selling information to the highest bidder?"

Indira deflated. "Guess not. What do you propose?"

Evelyn brightened. "Oh, I have a plan…"

"KNOCK, KNOCK!" Evelyn poked her head around Scott's office door. The man had his head down, his nose almost touching his laptop screen. Startled, his eyes widened. He recovered his composure and shoved his glasses up on his nose.

"What can I do for you?" he huffed, glowering at her. Not taking the hint, Evelyn closed the door behind her, breezed in and grabbed a chair.

"Actually, it's more of what I can do for you," she said, her voice low.

"Excuse me?" Scott removed his glasses and massaged the bridge of his nose. Evelyn hoped she'd given him a headache.

"I know." She tilted her head and smiled.

"You know?" A bead of sweat appeared at his hairline.

Evelyn nodded and scooched forward. She placed one hand on the desk, the other slipped into her pocket and withdrew a folded copy of the grant. "Recognize this? I do. And so did John. The miracle drug the tech bros of Silicon Valley are touting? The one they say they 'discovered?' I know it was developed here, in this lab...by you. And the only reason a person wouldn't want their name in journals the world over for discovering something so altruistic, so groundbreaking, is because of money. You developed it, understood what you had, and sold it to the highest bidder. These documents make it sound like your research went bust, but when I compared the two, I found they were identical. Your lab put the drug through its trials. You helped to develop a potential cure for a form of pediatric cancer. Tell me I'm wrong."

Sweat poured down Scott's face. "I don't know what you're talking about."

"No?" She pulled out her phone. "Well, I have the receipts." She showed him an email from Darius Thompson of Skylar Labs in California. One she'd found in John's files. She hadn't understood it at first, but now she did.

"What do you want?"

She shook her head. "I want my husband back. Short of that, I'd like you to confess."

He laughed. "First you accuse me of selling trade secrets and now you're insinuating I murdered John?" He stood and held his hand out. "May I see your phone? Are you recording this?"

Evelyn slid her phone out of her handbag and handed it to him. The phone was off.

Satisfied, he nodded. "Okay. Let's discuss this over tea. I was about to make myself a cup."

Evelyn nodded. "Sure, I'd love some."

He left. Evelyn glanced out into the hallway and caught

sight of Indira, who gave her the thumbs up. When Scott returned, he handed her the cup and sat. "Now, first can I just say, bravo. You and your husband are quite the pair. I offered to cut him in but he refused. If you're smart, you'll take the deal. Skylar made me very rich and I can be generous."

Evelyn sat tightlipped.

"Drink your tea," he commanded.

"What exactly did you do to my husband when he turned down your deal?" her voice wavered.

"I work in a lab. I know how to make death look natural." As he laughed, the door opened and campus security entered, accompanied by the local police. Scott sputtered.

Evelyn set her tea down on the desk. "Officers, you'll want to test this. I'm certain it will test positive for Oleander. I found some in his lab earlier today."

"How in the—?" Scott asked.

Evelyn pointed to Skelly, a decoration wearing a party hat that Indira had rolled into his office earlier, telling him it was for his birthday. The handbag on Skelly's arm held a recording device. While Evelyn hadn't trusted the skeleton before, he had her complete and total faith now.

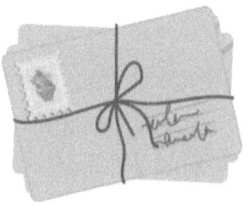

The Stork Brothers Thing

Daniel Fox

YOU MEET THE FERRY.

You get the mail delivery.

You get to sorting, and then you get to delivering.

Mary Nagata had been delivering the mail to Hard-scrabble Island's thirteen hundred or so residents since she'd been in her early twenties. She'd developed a system without even realizing it, and she was as regular as the tides. So when something slipped outside her way of doing things, she tended to notice. Even if she didn't notice her noticing, if you get what I mean.

Here's what happened. Mary was toolin' around in her van, doing the usual. It got to be about two o'clock, at which time Mary's brain usually tended to get a little on the sleepy side. So she stopped in at The Coffee Shop, which was the coffee shop's actual name. She'd been experimenting with different flavours, and that day she ordered what Edna, The Coffee Shop's owner, called a 'Little Richard.' It was a shot of espresso dumped into a cold Mexican cola and not only did the concoction chase away her sleepiness, the caffeine jolt nearly shot the top of her skull off.

It was then that Mary realized she had noticed something. She said, "Hey, where's Geraldine?"

Edna said, "That's what I'd like to know."

Normally, The Coffee Shop was this minor hurricane of sniping between Edna and her only employee, Geraldine Mast. They harped at each other pretty much every day because that's just what they did. It was the silence that Mary had not noticed she was noticing.

"She sick?"

"How should I know?"

"She didn't call in to say she'd be missing work?"

"If she did, I'd know if she was sick."

"Fair point. Well, I'm heading her way. Maybe I'll stick my nose in, see if she's okay."

"Tell her she's fired."

"You can't fire her."

"Why not?"

"Because she's like a sister to you."

"Cain and Abel were brothers and look how that turned out."

Mary laughed and went back to her rounds. She arrived at Geraldine's trailer around three that afternoon. The trailer was a handsome thing, permanently built up on a wooden base, with a nice wooden porch off the entrance. Mary didn't have any mail for Geraldine that day, but she hopped out of her white van all the same and went up onto the porch. She gave a knock at the door.

Nothing.

Just the breeze playing in the leaves of the trees. Maybe the sound of the surf coming in, real faint, off in the distance. A bird here and there. No Geraldine shuffling around in the trailer, though.

She tried the door. Found it unlocked. She opened it a crack.

"Hello? Gerry?"

Mary stepped inside.

Violence had been here. Books were scattered everywhere, looking like dead birds. Cushions had been cut open, displaying their guts. A vase had been smashed, its pieces crunching under Mary's sneakers. Every drawer had been yanked open and its contents scattered to the four winds. The old-fashioned rotary phone was on the floor, beeping a hang-me-up noise over and over again.

This time, Mary had no trouble at all noticing that something was wrong.

"THIS IS SERGEANT IBSEN."

"Hiya Sergeant, how's your day going?"

"Busy as a bee. Just helping out with the forest fires on the mainland, you know. Steering people away from travelling over if they can avoid it."

"Oh, shoot. I thought I was calling the type of RCMP who kept watch out here in the Gulf Islands."

"That's me, alright. These fires are just raging though, so the mainlanders needed some extra help. What can I do you for, Miss Nagata?"

"A lady here, Geraldine Mast, she didn't show up for work. I went by her trailer and I gotta tell ya, I haven't ever seen anything quite like it. Looks like an angry bear went right through there."

"Missing, is she?"

"I think there's a chance of it, yep. And in case you were going to ask, she's not on the crystal meth or that Fentanyl stuff or any such thing you can name. Not that I know, anyway."

"Okay, I'll try to boot it over to your island quick as I can. It just depends on if they figure they can let me go for the afternoon or not. In the meantime, if you hear anything about Geraldine, you call me at this number and let me know."

"That sounds just fine, Sergeant. Thank you."

"I appreciate your call. Keep your eyes and ears open."

MARY SPENT a good half hour going through all the papers and whatnot she found scattered across Geraldine's floor. The only surprise was a stack of real estate magazines, full of listings aimed at millionaires. They showed old, fancy high-ceilinged apartments in Paris. Ritzy homes that had balconies opening on the Mediterranean coastline. One magazine even listed castles for sale, seated on hills in green rolling European countrysides. Seemed Geraldine had a hankering for the high life that Mary hadn't known about, but you couldn't hardly blame a lady for that.

She still had mail to deliver and two more mailboxes to empty out on the island so she could get the outgoing mail on the afternoon ferry. She hopped back in her van and got rolling, staying on the lookout for Geraldine or anybody that might have seen her.

She stopped by the mailbox closest to Geraldine's trailer. It was an antique, tall, narrow box-shape with a pull-

slot for inserting letters, a stamped Canadian crest on a little metal plaque, two more stamped metal bits below saying 'Canada' and 'Post Office,' and a keyhole below that for the collection of outgoing mail by postal officers.

There were some new scratch marks and dents along the edge of the bottom door where postal workers retrieved the outgoing mail. Somebody had put effort into breaking into this old beast of a mailbox. She grabbed the handle of the lower door and pulled. It opened with a screech.

There were only a couple of envelopes in the bottom. That was normal. These days, most people chatted on the phone, emailed, text-messaged or used those video-call programs that Mary found annoying, because who wanted to get dolled up just to talk to somebody from work? If somebody had broken in to steal a letter, they had likely succeeded, given the state of the lower door and its busted lock. She hated to see it. Hardscrabble Island was virtually crime free. And for that crime to be aimed at an antique like this mailbox, well, it broke her heart a little.

It was then that Mary noticed two things (this was an A-plus day for Mary noticing stuff). First, one of the letters she had collected was from Geraldine and it was addressed to Edna at The Coffee Shop. Why the heck was Geraldine sending Edna a letter when they saw each other in the flesh most every day? Second, the bottom of the box was wonky. The floor of the mailbox was raised. She had never really paid attention to it before, but it was like someone had taken a metal box, the same red as the mailbox itself, flipped it upside down, and wedged it into the bottom of the mailbox, creating a false floor.

But someone else had noticed. And they had wrestled with the thing until that false floor came up. Mary reached in and pulled out the false floor box. It came out easy in her hand. Sometime, a long time ago from the looks of it, someone had added a hidden compartment to this mailbox. And today, someone else had discovered it. And whatever had been inside.

TECHNICALLY, Geraldine's letter was supposed to go through the system so that it could be registered. But it seemed kind of silly when Mary could hand the letter off to its recipient after a ten-minute drive. She returned to The Coffee Shop and had to wait in line, practically dancing in anticipation, as a tourist couple had Edna explain all the different coffee options before they ultimately gave their order.

Finally, she slapped the letter into Edna's hand. Edna glanced at it, grunted, tossed it onto a shelf behind the counter, and asked Mary what she wanted.

"I want you to read that letter."

"Why?"

"Because..." Mary realized her voice was amped up. She made an effort to lower her volume and tried again. "Because I think Geraldine is missing. I took a look in Geraldine's trailer. It's trashed."

"It's probably always trashed. She's a slob. I'm always after her to wipe the counters."

"No, I mean, it looks like someone was rooting through her stuff. A burglar."

Edna snorted. "Here? On the island? Are we importing them now?"

"It could have been a, you know..." She gave a sneaky

little nod over at the couple seated at a nearby table, "…tourist."

"We can hear you," said the woman.

"Now *I* want to hear about what's in the envelope," said the man. "And I don't even know who Geraldine is."

"Fine." Edna grabbed the envelope, ripped it open, and pulled out a lined yellow sheet of paper.

"Well?"

"She quits." Edna flapped the page. "She says I'm a rotten person to work for and she can't take me anymore and she doesn't want to work under the tyranny of a boss who wants her to show up on time and wash some coffee spoons now and again. I'm summarizing."

"That doesn't explain a busted-up trailer, does it?"

Edna shrugged. "She's burned her bridge here. Maybe she's burned all her bridges and was just in a hustle to get out off the island. There's a time when a person says, 'enough is enough' and they just blast off, like a rocket ship heading into orbit. You ask me, Geraldine is gone."

———

MARY STILL HAD a job to do, so she gathered the outgoing mail into a waterproof bin and took it down to the ferry dock. She arrived just as the ferry was pulling in, and she stood aside as a trickle of early-season tourists drove or walked off.

She took the bin of mail on board and handed it to Barry, a native Salish fella who had been working on this ferry maybe since the dawn of time. He had a thick head full of white hair pulled into a ponytail that went all the way down his back, which looked pretty snazzy contrasted to his blue ferry uniform jacket.

"Hey there, mail lady."

"Hey there yourself, ya handsome devil. Do you know Geraldine Mast?"

"Sure. Fiery red hair that's all wavy. Big..." Barry cupped his hands out in front of his chest.

"Yeah buddy, well spotted. Did she happen to head out on this morning's ferry?"

"She didn't."

"How about on yesterday's runs?"

"Nope. This is sounding mysterious. Something's up?"

"Maybe," said Mary, heading back onshore. "Maybe so."

The mail done, she drove herself back home. Mary had a log bungalow and a little plot of land that used to belong to her grandfather when he had been a young man. Many Japanese immigrants had worked land along the west coast of North America back then, and a lot of them had that land appropriated when they were removed and interred back in WWII. The British Columbia trust that held the land was supposed to give the plots back after the war, but they sold them instead, which was as dirty as it got. Ever since Mary had been a kid, she'd been focused on getting her grandpa's land back; and she did.

She was planning on setting up some fencing to try to keep out the deer. She got as far as pulling out the rolls of chicken wire to go between the upright posts when it just got to her. She couldn't leave the mystery alone.

She went back into her house and grabbed her phone but couldn't find where she had written down the sergeant's direct number. She had jotted it down on a piece of scrap paper instead of inputting it into her phone like a normal human being, and this is what she got as a result.

So she redialed the number for the Gulf Islands branch of the RCMP. A lady with a nice voice answered.

"Hiya. Mary Nagata here. I'm trying to get in touch with Sergeant Ibsen. If he's not too busy with the fires."

"Busy with the fires? How do you mean?"

"He's busy keeping people from heading over to where the forest fires are on the mainland."

"Don't think so. Just let me check for you real quick."

Mary looked out the window. Two deer were pushing over her rolls of chicken wire, clearly in an attempt to mock her.

"Miss Nagata?"

"I'm here."

"Sergeant Ibsen is on his usual marine patrol. You know those cute little black and white boats we have?"

"I sure do! They look like so much fun."

"Right? I hope to get out on them myself someday."

"You totally should. I bet it makes for a beautiful day, booting around the islands in one of those."

"I'm studying up to do field work."

"Well good luck to you!"

"Thank you so much! At any rate, yeah, none of us here have anything to do with the forest fires on the mainland. Do you still want me to put you in touch with the sergeant?"

IT TURNED OUT THAT NO, Mary didn't want to get in touch with Sergeant Ibsen. The bad feeling that had been in the pit of her stomach since she'd been to Geraldine's trailer got worse with the news that the sergeant had lied about his location.

She had the nice lady put her in touch with a constable, who started up a province-wide lookout for Geraldine. But British Columbia was a big province. There were a lot of coves and inlets a person could motor a boat into. Geraldine didn't own a boat of her own. Had she stolen one to make her big escape from the island?

To hell with it. Farming was not on her radar (sorry, Grandpa), and the deer were making a mockery of her fencing anyway. She went out, hopped back in her van, and began to prowl.

About halfway down the east coast, she started knocking on doors. She asked the same question over and over again: "Is your boat missing?"

She worked her way clockwise, going from house to house. The sun was on its way down by the time she finally made it all the way around the island's exterior. There wasn't a single boat missing. She was hot, hungry, and thirsty. She didn't feel like cooking, so she figured she'd head to one of the three restaurants on the island.

But first, she decided to take a stroll down to one of the pebble beaches and let the cooling air soothe her. She parked and walked down a short path through some long grass to a small beach known to all the locals, her feet skidding a little on the pebbles and small rocks. And what do you think she found but one of those cute little RCMP black and white boats anchored within wading distance of the shore.

A POLICE SERGEANT who had lied to her was on the island at the same time as someone went missing and their home got turned inside out. It could be a coincidence, but a cold twist in her gut was telling Mary otherwise.

Problem was, she had proof of absolutely nothing. What was she going to tell the RCMP? 'Hey, one of your fellas might have been romping around our island when he told me he was off stopping people from going to the fire-plagued mainland?' She was pretty sure they'd give her a 'That's super interesting, bud,' and then do absolutely nothing with the information. She needed proof that something was going on. *If* anything was going on. She played a timeline in her head:

1. Geraldine got fed up enough with Edna that she didn't bother showing up for work at The Coffee Shop.
2. Then, she wrote a scathing letter to Edna. She stuck it in the mail instead of hand-delivering it.
3. Next, she decided that maybe the letter wasn't such a good idea after all, so she broke into the antique mailbox to get it back.
4. In doing so, she also accidentally dislodged the false bottom. She opened it and found something inside.

Well alright, that all made sense. But how did a police guy learn about what Geraldine found?

Because she contacted him? Why would she do that? Because the thing she found had to do with some kind of crime. She thought she was reporting a crime. But that mailbox was *old*. The secret compartment was *old*. Was the crime old too?

Boom, off to the library.

THE LIBRARY, officially called The Hardscrabble Island Reading Centre, was a cute little log building with a central welcoming area and two little stubby sections off to the left and the right, the whole lot of it filling with light from the big windows. It was after hours and the library was closed, so Mary had to go down the street to the red brick house of Pauly Harrison, the head librarian, where she gave a polite knock on the door. He was intrigued with all Mary had to say on the topic of Geraldine's disappearance, and he added to the rush Mary was feeling by telling her that Geraldine had been in the library just before closing time yesterday.

Feeling like a couple of supersleuths, they piled into Mary's van and rushed back to the library.

"Okay," said Pauly, clapping his hands together. "Gerry was on one of the computers for a bit. Sending an email, I think. I can't help there, I don't know which email service she used, or her password. But I did help her dig up some island history. She wanted old newspaper clippings going back to the 1920s."

"We have newspapers going back that far?"

"Oh sure. I've got some going back to the gold rush in the 1800s. It's a hoot seeing how they wrote articles back then." He went into the back and quickly returned with two thick volumes the size of cutting boards. He dropped them on the reception counter with a thud. "She was looking through these."

They each took a volume and opened them up. The pages were plain paper, with old newspaper clippings glued to them. Mary had to admit that Pauly had been right, it *was* kind of a hoot to see the old-fashioned articles, fonts, and illustrations of yesteryear.

"Any idea of what we're looking for?" asked Pauly.

"I guess we'll know it when we see it."

Which they did, eventually. After a good half-hour of turning pages, Pauly grunted and said, "I'll bet this is it."

"How do you know?"

"Because someone, and by 'someone' I mean that rascal Geraldine, drew a little star next to this article. It figures. The Stork Brothers. They can't stop causing crime even though they've been gone nearly a hundred years"

"Who," inquired Mary, "were the Stork Brothers?"

PROHIBITION POOPED the party down in the United States from 1920 through 1933. There was alcohol aplenty in Canada, and not a legal drop in the States. Where such an imbalance existed, there was a chance to make some money.

The Stork Brothers were fishermen, tooling around the waters off Hardscrabble, and had themselves a fair-sized fishing boat. They decided to dip their toes into the whisky-running business. The thing was, they got into the illicit booze-running trade late, and a number of gangs had grown pretty strong by that point. These included ex-cop Roy Olmstead, 'The King of the Puget Sound Bootleggers';

the Reifel family out of Vancouver; Emmie-May Binns; the McCoy family, and a couple of other smaller gangs.

The Stork Brothers, Marcus and Reg, did pretty well underselling those established gangs. Enough so that the established gangs noticed their piggy banks getting a little lighter every month. Marcus and Reg became marked men. They hightailed it out of the west coast, never to be heard of again. Legend had it that they left a large portion of their fortune behind, buried somewhere on the island. Pauly remembered his own grandfather wandering around with a metal detector as a hobby, trying to find the location. Never turned up a red-hot dime.

"You know what I think?" Pauly said, wrapping up his tale. "I think maybe those Stork boys rigged up the mailboxes on the island like you said and used them as drop points for secret messages, telling clients where to find stashes of booze. But when they had to skedaddle off the island, they left one last message in that wrecked old mailbox of yours, with a map or directions stating where they had concealed that hidden fortune, intending to come back one day to retrieve it."

"Geraldine popped open the box," said Mary, "to take back her letter. But she also popped open that hidden compartment and found the Stork Brothers' last message. She forgot about retrieving her own letter and took that instead. For some reason I don't understand yet, she sent an email to the sergeant. And now he's here. But from the look of her trailer, they're not working together like she hoped. The sergeant trashed her home looking for the Stork Brothers' map or message because he either hasn't found Geraldine yet, or he *did* find her but can't get her to tell where X marks the spot."

"Either way," said Pauly, "I think our red-headed friend is in a heap of trouble."

PAULY GOT ON THE PHONE, called the RCMP and gave them the whole story. Mary took off running, climbed into her van and was on the move.

The question was—on the move to *where?*

Geraldine and Sergeant Ibsen hadn't been spotted along the coastline of the island. Mary would have come across someone who had seen them while she was hunting for missing boats. They were likely still on the island because no boats were missing, and the sergeant's boat was still out there by that pebble beach. Everybody she had talked to hadn't seen Geraldine, so she hadn't been near the 'downtown' area, the restaurants, the docks, or the tourist hot spots.

Good old Marcus and Reginald had been sneaky little booze runners. They probably had drop spots all over the island in little coves tucked away between big rocks. But would they hide their ultimate stash in places their criminal brethren knew about? Probably not. If Mary had been a criminal on the run from other scary crooks with hopes of returning one day to retrieve a jackpot, where would she hide it? Where was the last place other smugglers would think to look? She put the pedal to the metal and sped to the island's only church.

It was an all-denominational, tidy little brown one-storey building with a sharply peaked roof, white trim and a small bell tower sticking up like a periscope at one end. Mary didn't see any sign of activity on the church grounds.

She tried the door, found it locked. That didn't mean there wasn't anybody inside, though. So she grabbed a rock from the ankle-high stone border wall around the tiny parking lot, using it to batter at the door just above the lock until the wood cracked and she was able to push her way inside.

The air was still and quiet except for her breathing.

The pulpit or the altar or whatever you called the priesty area was to her immediate right. Eight pews with an aisle between them were to her left. There was a distinct lack of Geraldine or Sergeant Ibsen.

She noticed a door to the cellar opposite the entrance and gave it a push, snapping on the lights as she ran downstairs. She didn't know what exactly she intended to do if she had to confront a crooked police officer who likely had, you know, a *gun*, but that was a hurdle she would leap when she got to it.

The cellar was empty except for some lawn chairs and what looked like an old volleyball net. The floor was compacted dirt, the walls were stone, and none of it looked disturbed. So much for her big fat hunch.

She went back out, leaving a note to explain the broken door and her promise to pay for repairs.

It hit her that there was another place criminals would have wanted to avoid back in the day.

It was a museum now, but back in the Stork Brothers' time, it had been a jail.

MARY PARKED down the road from the museum just as the sun finally gave up the ghost for the day. The museum was tiny, only about the size of a moderate bedroom, with light-yellow clapboard walls and a couple of stone steps leading up to its front door. She looked through a window. She could see old agricultural tools inside, pictures of the interred WWII Japanese folk, Native art and implements, as well as pictures back from the Gold Rush days. That was about all that could fit.

It looked untouched. Mary had already busted one door today; she wasn't sure she wanted to pay for another. She tried the handle. It was locked. She put her ear to the door, heard nothing.

She grabbed a flashlight from the van and patrolled the grounds behind the little museum. A slow rise led up a rock slope. Climbing to the top, she could see the ocean past the trees to the east. She heard a muffled sound behind her. She spun around, sure she was about to get her fool self shot right through the heart.

She found a bald man in an RCMP uniform gagged, his hands handcuffed behind his back, tied to a tree with rope. Mary pulled off his gag.

"That lady is crazy," said Sergeant Ibsen.

MARY WAITED UNTIL PAULY, Edna and a couple of the other locals responded to her cell phone call for help before she untied the sergeant. He was eager to talk, admitting his guilt.

"I heard that the Stork Brothers' fortune was going to be found," said the Sergeant, "so, yep, yep, yep, I uh... yep, I leaped at 'er. I know Geraldine from way back. We dated when I first joined the force and started patrolling these waters. We stayed in touch off and on. And then yesterday, a call from heaven. Or so I thought. She'd found this letter saying where the Storks had hidden their big stash. But she wouldn't tell me where, at first. I admit I got a bit testy and made a mess of her home."

He led the locals to a small opening in the rock under the clinging roots of a birch tree.

"It was in there, sure enough. A big metal box in an old oilskin bag. Full of old bills. Not sure how Geraldine plans to convert those without getting caught. But as I was hauling that box out, she yanked my gun," he pointed at his empty holster, "and, well...that's that story told."

"How come she called you at all?" said Edna. "Why not just grab it for herself?"

"Aw," said the Sergeant. "She didn't really call for me. She called for my boat. You-all would have noticed a boat missing if she took one of yours. So I brought an outside boat and anchored it where none of you could see it. I guess I'm a double fool 'cause I left the keys right in the ignition. She's long gone by now."

"Maybe not,' said Mary. "I saw your boat earlier today. Not only that, but I took off my shoes and socks and waded on out to her and..." She fished in her pocket and pulled out a set of keys attached to a floatable bob. "She's not going anywhere in that thing."

———

THE LOCALS GRABBED their cell phones at that point and started making calls, telling everyone to go check on their boats. Sure enough, Geraldine was found untying the Fortiers' twenty-five-footer from their dock, using only the thin moonlight as her guide. The showdown consisted of

Geraldine telling Michael Fortier to stand back as she had a gun, and Michael Fortier, who had known Geraldine his whole life, asking if she would really shoot him. Geraldine confessed that no, she thought maybe she couldn't do such a thing, and gave up.

All that old money, along with Sergeant Ibsen and Geraldine, got handed over to other RCMP officers who came across in their own cute little black and white police boats. The money, of course, was too old to be put back into circulation, but it was deemed a shame to just destroy it since it had such a rich history buried in its folds. So the bulk of it ended up in some RCMP warehouse until some-body could figure out just what to do with it.

All except one crisp ten-dollar bill, framed in glass, which you can see to this very day in the Hardscrabble Island Museum.

Stamped, Sealed and Duval

Denise Landry

MARC DUVAL SAT by the window, watching the early sunlight spill over the worn cobblestone streets of Petit-Champlain. The scent of fresh bread and coffee wafted up from the cafe below, mingling with the crisp air drifting in through his open window. His grandfather, Simon, had once walked these same streets, delivering letters and packages with a steadfast dedication that Marc had always admired. Simon had been more than a postman; he had been a storyteller, spinning tales about lost letters, lovers reunited, and secrets carried in envelopes as if the mail itself had a heartbeat. Marc looked over his own stack of mail on his desk. It was the ordinary bills, advertisements, a postcard from an old colleague. And something unusual.

A half-opened letter, addressed simply to 'M. Duval.' The envelope was creased, as though it had travelled far, passing through many hands before arriving at his door by mistake. Since it was half unsealed, curiosity got the best of him. He opened the aged envelope. The paper was also aged—edges worn, the ink smudged in places.

A single line was written on it: '*I hope you enjoyed the trip as much as I did.*' Signed by '*My Love.*'

Marc frowned. The handwriting was elegant but unfamiliar. He turned the envelope over, checking for a return address. Nothing. Just an old postage mark from Los Angeles. It was mislabeled to Canada. Strange.

Then, his eyes fell upon the stamp attached to the letter. It was unlike any he'd seen before. The design was an image of a medieval queen, standing solemnly among forest shadows. Marc tilted his head, studying it closely. It was upside down. Was the image printed incorrectly?

Becoming more curious by the minute, he tucked the letter into his jacket pocket and wheeled his wheelchair toward the elevator. As the doors slid open, he pulled out his phone, dialling Isabelle's number. "Isabelle, it's Marc. I just got the strangest letter. Meet me at the cafe. I think we've got something interesting."

Isabelle Fournier hurried over to the cafe. She ordered coffee as she examined the envelope, letter, and stamp. She was fascinated with it. She and Marc shared the same love for postal artifacts, documents, and lost treasures—she as a seasoned postal worker, he as a leading historian of postal history, lecturing across Canada. They had met at a philately exhibition. Since then, her encyclopedic knowledge of postal anomalies made her an invaluable resource whenever Marc stumbled upon something unusual. He now hoped that she could help with this curiosity.

Isabelle held the letter between her fingers, studying the stamp carefully. She narrowed her eyes, flipping it under the warm cafe light. "This looks familiar, Marc," she murmured. "I swear I've seen something like this before, in the archives."

Marc leaned forward. "Postal archives?"

She nodded. "Yes. There was a case, something about an incredibly valuable misprint. It was documented decades ago."

Marc felt his pulse quicken. "Then let's check."

The cobblestone streets posed no challenge to Marc's wheelchair or his spina bifida. He glided smoothly between uneven stones, nodding to familiar shop owners as they made their way toward the postal archives. Inside the building, Isabelle checked if the letter had been processed through regular mail systems. Yes, but it had passed through a series of mailing errors. It should've gone to dead letters, not randomly to Marc. Isabelle then took Marc to the archives housing a wealth of historical records dating back centuries. Inside, rows upon rows of documents rested in dimly lit cabinets. Isabelle guided Marc toward a specific section of misprints and anomalies.

They searched until Isabelle let out a quiet gasp. "This is it," she whispered, pulling out an old catalogue entry. "The *Inverted Gwenieve*, a misprinted stamp depicting a medieval queen, printed upside down. It was stolen from a collector years ago."

Marc scanned the details. A theft. A missing piece of history. They looked at each other. Marc pulled out his phone again. "We need Felix. If there's anyone who can track the origins of this letter, it's him."

Felix Tremblay, Marc's investigative journalist friend, answered after the second ring.

"You sound urgent," he said.

"I might've stumbled onto something big," Marc replied drumming his fingers on a table. "Have you heard of the *Inverted Gwenieve*?"

Felix let out a low whistle searching the online news archives. "Rare misprint. Stolen decades ago from a collector, Madame Bernard. Never recovered." He didn't hesitate. "Send me photos. I'll dig through auction records, black-market dealings, anything that traces its route."

MARC, Isabelle, and Felix gathered around a corner table at the cafe. Felix leaned forward. "Alright. This is what I found." He flipped open his laptop, showing an old newspaper clipping from 1986. A headline read: 'Rare Stamp Stolen—The *Inverted Gwenieve* Vanishes Without a Trace.'

The article detailed the theft from collector Madame Colette Bernard, an incident that had rocked philatelic circles. The stolen stamp had been considered priceless and despite rumours of black-market dealings, it had never resurfaced at any official auctions. "We should return the stamp to Madame Bernard immediately." Marc and Isabelle agreed.

"I will track her down." Felix nodded. "It'll make a great story for the paper."

Then the cafe door swung open and a tall, well-dressed man entered. He purposely scanned the room before heading straight for their table. "Mr. Duval."

Marc glanced up. Isabelle and Felix exchanged looks.

Beaumont, a private investigator, pulled a business card from his coat pocket and set it down between them. "I represent a concerned party who's willing to compensate you generously for the stamp, should you choose to sell."

Marc raised an eyebrow, crossing his arms. "It's not

mine to sell. We are going to track down the rightful owner and return it to her."

Beaumont tilted his head slightly, "My client will pay you double what the stamp is worth."

Marc's tone sharpened. "And who, exactly, is this 'concerned party?' "

Beaumont gave a neutral smile but didn't answer. Instead, he simply pushed the card closer. "If you change your mind, call me." Then with a nod, he turned and exited the cafe, leaving an uneasy silence between the three friends.

Felix scoffed, shaking his head. "That was weird."

Isabelle frowned. "Who tries to buy stolen property with that much confidence?"

Marc stared at the card. Someone unknown knew they had the stamp. And whoever it was, they wanted it for themselves badly.

THE NEXT DAY, Felix slid his laptop across the cafe table, pulling up an old investigative report. His voice was measured yet laced with intrigue. "Madame Bernard didn't just lose the stamp. She lost everything. The scandal surrounding her assumed her lover, Olivier Coeur, conned her into letting him disappear with the stamp. Humiliated, she was forced into hiding. It destroyed her reputation in collector circles. She never recovered."

Marc frowned, scanning the screen. "And she passed away?"

Felix nodded. "Two years ago. Since then, her estate

has been quietly trying to reclaim what was lost, including the stamp. Officially, it belongs to them now."

Marc exhaled slowly. "That feels cold," Marc said. "She spent her life chasing this stamp, and now it's just another item in an inheritance file?"

Isabelle pressed her lips together, thoughtful. "It was personal for her."

Felix continued to read from his laptop screen, "Olivier, nicknamed 'Silverheart,' is an older man who has sweet talked and pretended to love many men and women so he could con them out of their property and wealth over the years."

Isabelle couldn't believe what she was hearing. "Poor people."

Then, as if from nowhere, a strange woman appeared. Margot Duval stood poised, her sharp gaze locking onto Marc at the table. Her presence demanded attention.

"That stamp doesn't belong to Madame Bernard's estate," she announced, her tone firm but controlled. "It belongs to us."

Marc sat back, measuring her words. "And who is *us*?"

Margot pulled a folded slip of paper from her bag, smoothing it onto the table. The auction receipt was aged but intact, dated years ago, listing the *Inverted Gwenieve* among the purchases. "My husband, 'My Love' in that letter, bought it at a private auction in Los Angeles. We didn't know it had been stolen." Her voice carried an edge. Conviction, frustration. "But we paid for it, fair and square. That stamp is ours." She then giggled. "My silly husband mixed up the stamps one day. And he put *The Inverted Gwenieve* on a letter to me when I was on vacation. I've been frantically searching for it ever since."

Marc gave the 'My Love' letter to her. She had proven that it was hers. But he held the envelope with the stamp tightly. "You can fight for ownership of the stamp with the Bernard estate when we return it." Margot stormed away, obviously upset.

Marc exhaled slowly, his thoughts tangling between the conflicting claims of Margot and Beaumont. He exchanged a glance with Isabelle and Felix. So who did the stamp truly belong to?

LATER THAT NIGHT, the silence of Marc's apartment was shattered by the sound of drawers being ripped open and papers rustling frantically. He jolted awake, his pulse hammering. For a split

second, he thought it was a dream. Then came the unmistakable sound of objects hitting the floor, his desk being overturned. Someone was tearing his place apart.

Marc shouted, his voice raw with urgency as he scrambled into his wheelchair, hands gripping the armrests tightly. The intruder must have heard him because suddenly, the chaos stopped.

Marc wheeled out the door and toward the elevator, heart pounding. As he reached for the call button, footsteps thundered down the stairs quickly. The front door to the cafe stood wide open, hinges splintered. He called the police. Then he noticed an older man in a car across the street looking at him, who drove off when the police came. Marc stared at the door wreckage, catching his breath. They hadn't taken anything. No valuables. No electronics. So what were they looking for? The stamp? Luckily, Isabelle had the stamp secured in a post office safe, ready for further investigation.

Morning came and Marc wheeled through the clutter of his apartment. Isabelle and Felix worked quickly, setting overturned furniture back in place, sweeping up splinters from the busted doorframe.

Marc ran a hand over the dented edge of his desk. "I'll help pay for the cafe door," he said, voice tight. "Maybe this was my fault?"

Felix shook his head. "You didn't invite whoever did this."

THEN, another envelope. No name. No postmark. Just plain paper, slipped through his door.

Marc unfolded it, his stomach twisting as he read the message: 'Don't trust Margot! She's a scammer!'

His jaw tightened. Of course he didn't trust her. But this—this anonymous warning—felt like a game. An unfair shove, pushing him toward someone else's agenda. And that angered him. Marc had questions and Margot wasn't easy to find. But Beaumont—he had his card. Marc called Beaumont. Beaumont answered, his voice unusually tense.

"Duval."

Marc didn't waste time. "Did you or your client, who wants the stamp, break into my apartment last night?"

"No! My client was in his hotel room all night. I left him there myself. I went to my office and found my own problems."

Marc frowned. "What do you mean?

Beaumont exhaled sharply. "My office was broken into last night also."

Marc sat up straighter. "Same night as my place?"

"Same night." Beaumont's tone darkened. "Whoever it was, they were looking for something. Something that we are both interested in. I think it is time you meet my client, Jason Bélanger."

Marc agreed to the meeting.

LATER, Jason sat hunched over his coffee, eyes darting toward the cafe entrance every few moments. He looked worn down by something deeper than frustration.

Marc studied him carefully. Beaumont turned to Jason. "Tell him about your grandmother."

Jason sighed, rubbing his temple. "Vivienne Bélanger. She was supposed to have a copy of the stamp, promised to her years ago."

Felix leaned in. "Why?"

Jason exhaled. "She was the model for it. Her boyfriend was the artist. He worked on the design and she posed for it, the medieval queen. She was supposed to get a copy as a keepsake. But then the mistake happened: the first printing was inverted. It became a collector's item overnight. Suddenly, she couldn't have it anymore."

Isabelle frowned. "Because it was too valuable?"

"I guess," Jason shrugged. "I've been tracking down copies to give to my grandmother. I never had money to buy one." He then apologized to Beaumont for lying about his money situation. "Then I ran into Margot, a stamp expert, she said. She said she could track down the stolen stamp for me."

Felix leaned forward. "And instead?"

Jason gave a bitter laugh. "She scammed me. Took the little money my family had, promised connections, led me in circles. I got nothing. And then I saw her outside the cafe with some older man."

Marc's stomach dropped. "I wonder if it was the man I saw outside my apartment last night."

Jason continued. "That's when I got nervous. Whatever Margot's up to, it's bigger than just conning me."

Beaumont's expression was tight. "I wouldn't have handled this case the way I did if I had known about this. I would have protected you. Hunted her down and gotten your money back."

Marc sat back, processing everything. This stamp was more than a relic. It was personal. Broken promises. A lost piece of history, not just a legal dispute. And now it had landed in his hands. He wished he could just give Jason the *Inverted Gwenieve*, but he couldn't.

Marc and Isabelle went to the post office. They clicked open the safe and Isabelle carefully pulled out the stamp. Marc sat across from her, hands resting on his knees, staring at the tiny artifact that had started everything. A mistake. A mystery. A threat.

Isabelle slid it across the table to him. "You really think that you can keep that secure until we return it to the estate lawyers?"

Marc exhaled slowly, pressing his fingers against the edge of the envelope. "I hope so."

FELIX LEANED AGAINST THE WALL, arms crossed. "You still think you should hand it over to Madame Bernard's estate?"

Marc hesitated. The estate wanted closure. Jason wanted justice. Margot wanted money and power. And Marc wanted answers. Marc and Felix went back to the cafe to talk to Jason. Isabelle was going shopping with friends. As soon as Marc and Felix met Jason, Felix's phone buzzed.

Felix's voice sharpened as he read the message. "My co-worker found something."

Marc leaned in. "Found what?"

Felix lifted his laptop, pulling up an old newspaper clipping, yellowed, dated, barely intact. But the photo was clear. An original painting. Vivienne Bélanger, immortalized in oil in an obscure gallery, tucked away in a forgotten collection.

Jason stood behind them, breath catching in his throat. "That's her."

Marc turned to him, seeing the happiness in his expression. He could never have the stamp, but this, this was a part of her that he could reclaim.

Jason unclenched his jaw. "Where is it?"

Felix flipped the screen shut. "The gallery still owns it. You can buy it."

Jason sat back, deep in thought. He had a chance to give his grandmother what she had lost, if he only had the money. But before anyone could process the information, Marc's phone vibrated.

Beaumont's voice was tense. "Duval. You're never going to believe this."

Marc frowned. "What now?"

Beaumont let out a sharp breath. "The older man from the cafe? The one watching you? That's Olivier Coeur."

Marc stiffened.

Felix swore under his breath, "Silverheart."

Beaumont continued. "Yesterday when we left the cafe, I went around and busted in some doors myself. I banged on some nasty heads. And I confronted him. Pushed him. He played dumb, but the second I cornered him about the stamp, the mask slipped. Then he ran off before I could grab him and take him to the police."

Marc ran a hand through his hair. "That means Margot was with him. She's not working alone."

Beaumont's voice darkened. "She's not just scamming people, she's in deep." He ended the conversation.

Then, a second buzz.

Marc looked down at his phone. A text. Marc's stomach dropped. A photo. Isabelle, bound, sitting stiffly on the back seat of a car.

Then, the message: *The stamp. In exchange for her.* From Margot.

Marc's pulse hammered. Felix cursed. Jason clenched his fists. Marc informed Beaumont.

Beaumont snapped into motion. "We handle this carefully."

Marc swallowed hard. "How?"

Beaumont straightened. "We set the meet. We bait them. And we make damn sure they don't walk away."

THEY ARRIVED at a dimly lit warehouse. The sound of distant traffic. The hush of late-night air. Marc wheeled forward, Beaumont close beside him. Felix and Jason stayed back, keeping a sharp lookout.

Olivier and Margot stood waiting. Isabelle sat near them, unharmed but scared.

Margot's lips curled. "Smart. You came."

Marc held up the envelope. "You want the stamp? Here it is."

Olivier stepped forward, eyes gleaming. "Hand it over."

Marc tightened his grip, voice steady. "You first."

Olivier released Isabelle and she ran frantically into Felix's arms.

Beaumont was ready, watching for the moment when everything would snap.

And it did. Lights flooded the warehouse, red and blue flickering against steel beams. Officers swarmed. Chaos erupted. Olivier lunged but Beaumont was faster, grabbing his wrist, twisting him into submission.

Margot bolted, heels clacking against concrete, but Jason blocked her, forcing her to stumble. Police arrested Margot and Olivier. Marc wheeled back, heart pounding. It was over.

THE ESTATE WAS GIVEN the stamp, closing the file on that issue. Jason got his money back. Enough to pay Beaumont's fees, buy the painting and restore his grandmother's legacy. The newspaper ran the full story. Everyone enjoyed seeing Marc's name in print, reading about a mystery unraveling and a scandal exposed. Felix toasted them at the cafe. Isabelle smiled, despite everything. Beaumont proudly shook Marc's hand for a job well done.

MARC EMBARKED on a fruitful speaking tour. He delivered a captivating lecture on the now famous stamp and painting, weaving together history, intrigue, and the deeply personal stories behind them. He spoke of the stolen artifact and the painting's long journeys. How they had eluded collectors, broken trust and stirred greed, only to finally bring closure in ways no one had expected. The audience hung on his words, absorbing the strange idea that two simple things could wield such power.

Weeks later, Marc returned home, still reflecting on the twists and turns that had led him here. As he reached for his mail, a wry smile appeared on his lips. He flipped through the

envelopes, taking an extra moment to make sure that everything was stamped, sealed, and sent to the right M. Duval.

A Letter from the Past

Andrea Tillmanns

IT ALL STARTED QUITE HARMLESSLY.

The sports centre that had been built twenty years ago on a meadow near the edge of the city had long since fallen into disuse. What originally seemed like a good idea had soon turned into a financial bottomless pit when it became clear that hardly anyone wanted to pay the required court fees for tennis, squash, and badminton. The first operator had long since given up and sold the centre at a loss, while another operator filed for bankruptcy after a few years. Since then, the halls and tennis courts had remained untapped.

The city council had only been waiting for a good reason to have the facility demolished, and this reason had now been found: the old secondary school building could no longer be used with a clear conscience; it kept raining into the classrooms, many windows were leaking and the heating and sanitary facilities also urgently needed to be replaced. According to an expert opinion, a new building on the grounds of the sports centre would make more financial sense, even if many parents complained about the location—on average, students would have to travel further to school. But there was no alternative; the few building plots closer to the city centre would have been far too expensive for the indebted city.

It was only when the excavators were already rolling in to demolish the sports centre that a journalist from the Sandhome News noticed that a time capsule had been sunk into one of the foundations during construction: a small, airtight metal box in which people had placed photos, letters, or other items of importance. Using old newspaper photos, the journalist was able to pinpoint the exact location of the time capsule. She wrote an article about it and many curious people quickly turned up at the site to view the historical container. Some of them remembered having put something in it themselves, which now made them a little uncomfortable—obviously nobody had expected the time capsule to reappear after only twenty years. The newspaper article at the time spoke of fifty to a hundred years before the metal box would be accessed.

This is probably why many people were of the opinion that the time capsule should simply be placed back intact into the new foundations. But they didn't get their way. And so, in the end, a large crowd stood at the barrier around the construction site when the time capsule was recovered. The police secured the work as a precaution, as anonymous threatening letters had promised dire consequences if the capsule were opened. The press was allowed to approach and took lots of photos of the completely unspectacular, slightly rusty box, which were published in all the regional newspapers the next day. And everything was still quite harmless.

THAT BEGAN to change when the capsule was finally opened during a press conference at the town hall. Using the old newspaper photo of the time capsule's closing, an attempt had been made to bring in the people involved at the time, which was largely successful—one man had since emigrated, one woman had died in an accident, and another man could not be identified as his face was half covered and the caption did not mention any names. At the request of the press, the others posed for a current picture in the same order as in the original before the box was finally opened.

First, the photos that various people had placed in the time capsule were taken out and carefully photographed by the press. Most of them showed young people engaged in sports or celebrating; there were class photos and pictures of graduation ceremonies. The mayor held up some CDs that had been more or less current twenty years ago and made those present smile while holding cuddly toys. These finds were also photographed by the press. Finally, all that remained were the letters, which the mayor handed out to the press representatives to read. It took him a few minutes to answer more questions until an older journalist spoke up. "This letter here is...unusual," she said. "Mr. Mayor, can you please read it yourself? I'm going to publish it in tomorrow's edition of the Sandhome News and I don't want the authenticity of the content to be questioned."

And so it began.

The letter was unsigned; from the handwriting, it could be assumed that it had been written by a woman. The author claimed that a child in her neighbourhood had either been abducted by aliens and brought back changed, or he was a changeling—in any case, the child was no longer the same as in the first weeks of his life.

Of course, this theory obviously came from a rather confused person, and in a medium-sized town like Sandhome, there were more than enough people to whom such crude statements could be attributed. Nevertheless, the mayor also had a strange feeling when he read the letter. Perhaps there was a small spark of truth in these confused accusations?

In any case, the story made big waves after it was published the following day. On social media, there were the obligatory discussions between believers in UFOs and followers of the changeling theory, in which the question of the mysterious letter's author was repeatedly interspersed.

The comments on the Sandhome News website were much more rational. Some believed they recognized the handwriting in the short excerpt from the letter that the newspaper had printed; others discussed which of their neighbours might be confused enough to write such a letter. And still others concentrated on the real question: which infant at the time, who must now be twenty, perhaps twenty-one years old, was involved?

"There's actually not that much choice," Margaret remarked as she threaded the next yarn for her embroidery work. The story of the time capsule letter was also the number one topic at the weekly needlework meeting at the community centre. "Twenty years ago, there were already around sixty thousand inhabitants in Sandhome. If we roughly estimate that the average age now is around seventy-five, and if we assume that the child in question was no more than six months old, then there should be around four hundred people who could be implicated." Margaret's decades of experience as a primary school teacher came in handy when doing such calculations—she always said that primary school teachers could answer all of life's important questions.

"And how are you going to motivate them all to take a DNA test?" Patricia asked. As a former bank employee, she knew that people could be complicated.

"And their parents would also have to take part, of course," added Marie. "If they're still alive at all." She had been a housewife and mother all her life, had ended up caring for her parents and eventually her husband, and now she was slowly starting to do something for herself. Even if it was just crocheting with her friends for the time being.

"But the matter has to be investigated," Margaret insisted. "You can't just let accusations like that lie."

"And what should we do about it?" Patricia was her usual realistic self. "Do you want to write a letter to the editor of the newspaper to get things moving?"

"That would be a good start," Margaret replied. "It would also be good to find out who put something in the time capsule back then—was it just the people who can be seen in today's newspaper photo from the press conference, or were others involved?"

"Some of the people in the photo from back then couldn't be reached," Marie interjected, who had already read the online edition of the Sandhome News that morning. "So they are among the suspects. One of them has emigrated. Isn't that suspicious?"

Patricia frowned. "I don't really see any connection between emigration and crazy theories about switched children," she said. "Besides, we have no way of finding out. That's a matter for the police."

"Or the press, if the police don't do anything," Margaret remarked. "So, what exactly do we put in the letter to the editor?"

———————

THEY FINALLY AGREED that in the letter to the editor, they would ask the press and the police to take up the case to make sure that there really was no crime. At the same time, they also called on the people of Sandhome who were involved with the time capsule to contact the newspaper and share their memories to help solve the mystery surrounding the letter.

As the three of them had hoped, the letter was printed in the Sandhome News the very next day, and just one day later there were countless replies. As an exception, Margaret, Patricia and Marie met again on Friday to sort through all the information. The community centre had a colour printer and a large cork board on which they could now pin all the printouts, together with handwritten comments. Marie took care of the social media, where, as expected, there was little meaningful information, while the other two gathered the facts from the letters to the editor in the Sandhome News and the online comments. Conveniently, the Sandhome News had also reproduced the old photo of the time capsule being set in concrete in an earlier report on the construction site, so they now had a basis for finding the people who had been involved at the outset.

"But there must have been many more people involved," Marie interjected. "A former teacher writes here that her secondary school class at the time was also asked to put something in the capsule together. If she remembers correctly, it was probably a CD—with very strange music."

"Back then, there was nothing but strange music," Patricia remarked, "but let's stick to the people you can see in the picture for now. The school classes probably contributed things like music or stuffed animals, not strange letters."

Six people in the old picture were also in the new one, where they were identified. "They all look friendly, surely they have nothing to do with this weird letter," Marie pondered. "Otherwise, they wouldn't have turned up at the press conference where the contents of the time capsule were to be shown."

"If they had stayed away for no good reason, they would have made themselves even more suspicious," Margaret replied. "What about the emigrant?"

"He's been living in Australia for twelve years," Marie knew. "He doesn't seem to have noticed any of the hustle and bustle here; at least I haven't read any reaction from him to all the online discussions."

"Maybe he just doesn't read the news from Sandhome," Patricia interjected. "I'm sure there are more exciting things to experience in Australia."

After a brief discussion about the current heat wave in eastern Australia and whether it would be possible to travel the world at their age, the women refocused. "What about this man you can't really recognize?" asked Margaret. "Are there any clues?"

"The then principal of a vocational school," reported Marie. "He posted on the internet and complained that he hadn't been invited to the press conference. He certainly wouldn't have written such confused letters."

"That only leaves one woman who wasn't there this time," said Margaret, sticking a removable arrow over the person in the old photo.

"She couldn't have come, she's dead," Patricia remarked.

"But that doesn't rule out the possibility that she wrote the letter back then," Margaret replied.

They were silent for a while. "What did she actually die of?" Marie finally asked. "She doesn't look that old in the earlier photo."

No one could answer that. Maybe the newspaper editors knew. After a brief discussion, Margaret finally agreed to call the Sandhome News. After all, primary school teachers could do almost anything...perhaps even get information from journalists.

After some initial difficulties, she was eventually put through to Ms. Engels, the editor who had accidentally received the letter at the press conference with the reference to the switched child. Ms. Engels also found the topic exciting, but didn't really have time to deal with the unanswered questions surrounding the letter. "On the other hand," she finally said, "the topic really does seem to interest our readers..." She finally promised to do a little research.

In fact, the lead article in the Sandhome News the next day was unusually lurid: 'Assassination attempt? What does the death of Sandra B. have to do with the switched child?'

"Probably nothing," Margaret mumbled as she pulled the newspaper out of the letterbox and took it to the dining table to read over breakfast. Nevertheless, the article that Ms. Engels had written was not uninteresting—this Sandra

B. had been an alternative practitioner, one of the people looking after the time capsule at the time, and she died in a hit-and-run accident around nineteen years ago. Perhaps she had actually placed the mysterious letter in the time capsule, and perhaps she hadn't let up after that and told her confused stories one too many times? Of course, it could all be pure coincidence, but Margaret met with Patricia and Marie again in the community centre to discuss these new developments.

It was presumably this article that prompted the police to begin their investigation. Apart from general information, there was nothing in the newspaper for a few days and the speculation on the usual social media calmed down a little. And so it was a seemingly innocuous comment in a letter to the editor that brought new momentum to the story at the beginning of the following week. 'It is strange that another child disappeared in the neighbouring town at the same time as the alleged swap,' wrote the unnamed author of the letter to the editor. 'I wonder if the alleged aliens had a hand in that too?'

OVER THE NEXT FEW DAYS, Margaret, Patricia and Marie met daily at the community centre to keep up with the latest news. Of course, no one really believed in aliens, but the police drew a perfectly logical conclusion from the disappearance of the other child in the neighbouring town: had someone abducted this child to pass it off as their own? If that were the case, they would find out with a large-scale genetic test.

Since the police knew the date of the abduction, they

initially invited around two hundred young people and their parents to be tested; slightly fewer than Margaret had initially estimated. A good hundred of those invited had themselves tested; for almost a dozen, the results led to moderate family crises, as the children had not known until then that they were adopted, or the fathers only now learned that they were not the biological fathers. However, none of this was suspicious in terms of possible child abduction.

In the meantime, the parents of the child who had disappeared twenty years ago were repeatedly seen on television, initially only in the local news, soon also nationally. The mother still seemed deeply sad, while the father had obviously come to terms with what had happened. Margaret noticed his expensive watch and tailored suit— perhaps his way of compensating for the loss. And so it was the mother who kept talking about the hope of getting her lost son back. But the father of the kidnapped boy also made it clearer with every television appearance that he was anything but well. Margaret sometimes had the feeling that he was finding it increasingly difficult to keep up the façade and not collapse under the weight of this tragedy.

"A boy, then," she murmured and made a note to that effect on their pinboard, which they always hid under an inconspicuous knitted blanket between their meetings. Patricia had started the blanket a long time ago and still hadn't finished. "That still leaves about fifty potentially abducted boys and their parents missing from the DNA test."

"But it's still voluntary," remarked Marie, who, as usual, had already scoured the internet on the subject that morning. "Anyone who hasn't had a test before will probably not do it now."

It didn't take long for the police to come up with new figures: there remained forty-six young men who were the right age and had not turned up for the test. Some of them no longer lived in the region and obviously had no great interest in being tested. Others showed photos of themselves and their parents on social media and asked whether there could really be the slightest doubt that they were their parents' sons, and indeed, the resemblance to the respective fathers was often unmistakable.

Things became quieter again and Margaret, Patricia and Marie began to meet less frequently. This changed all at once when, around three weeks after the initial press conference, they read the headline on the front page of the Sandhome News: 'Father of abducted baby dead—another hit-and-run accident.'

They immediately agreed that two hit-and-run accidents in connection with abducted or switched children could no longer pass as coincidence. Ms. Engels formulated this somewhat more cautiously in her editorial, but of course she also saw the connections and asked the relevant questions: who could the man now killed have harmed? Had he found the kidnapper at the time? But how, when the police were in the dark about the abduction and didn't even know for sure whether there was a connection with the mysterious letter from the time capsule?

"What else do we know?" Patricia pondered aloud. "We have this Sandra B., who was killed in the accident and may have written the letter. She must have known the possibly switched child well; maybe she lived in the neighbourhood? Do we know where she lived?"

The three of them searched through the relevant newspaper clippings again, but there was no mention of the district, let alone the street where the woman had lived.

"Besides, this is probably the second murder with a car —it's not exactly the cheapest way to kill someone," Marie remarked. "We've always had to save up for a new car for a long time... we wouldn't have been able to afford major repairs, let alone a second car to run over unpleasant people."

"The recently killed father of the kidnapped boy seemed to earn quite well," Margaret reflected. "Even if that doesn't fit with the question of who might have run him over," she added quickly. "Still, do we know what he did for a living?"

"Sales assistant in a supermarket," said Marie, who was well informed as always.

"So how did he get a Patek Philippe watch?" Margaret asked in amazement and, noticing the looks on her friends' faces, added: "As a primary school teacher, you quickly learn to assess your pupils' homes."

"How much does a watch like that cost?" asked Marie.

"You could have bought a few small cars with that," Margaret replied.

They looked at each other. "Follow the money," muttered Patricia, who loved reading crime novels. "Did he get the money from his murderer?"

"Blackmail?" Margaret frowned. "How was that supposed to work? What did he know that was worth a lot of money and has now led to his death?"

They looked at each other and at that moment, they were probably all thinking the same thing. Margaret finally reached for her cell phone and called Ms. Engels from

Sandhome News. After a few introductory sentences, she got to the point. "We believe that the baby was not abducted, but sold," she said. "And whoever bought it must have been quite rich and lived near Sandra B. or at least had frequent contact with her."

Ms. Engels took such a deep breath that Patricia and Marie could hear it too. Then Margaret explained exactly how the three women had come up with this idea. "And you mean that the father of the allegedly abducted baby wanted to clear the air and was therefore killed?" she asked. "What about the mother?"

"She doesn't know anything," Margaret answered immediately, and Marie added: "Mothers would never do something like that."

THERE WAS no new headline the next day, nor for the next two days. Presumably, Ms. Engels did her research before publishing such an outrageous story. In fact, the Sandhome News was not even the first to report that two suspected murders and a faked kidnapping had been solved. Margaret immediately phoned Patricia and Marie when she heard in the local news credits about the press conference that was to deal with solving all the mysteries surrounding the time capsule. Most of what the police announced there, the three had already suspected: the allegedly abducted boy had grown up under the name Daniel with another family, right next door to the house of Sandra B. His foster mother, Mrs. W., had suspected nothing. After the birth of her own son, she had spent several months in a clinic suffering from severe depression. When her biological son died of sudden infant death syndrome, Mr. W. didn't have the heart to tell his wife; instead, he had bought the very similar-looking son from one of his employees for a lot of money and buried his own dead son in the woods.

Until then, Margaret could still understand what Mr. W. had done, even though he had caused Daniel's biological mother unspeakable suffering. But she couldn't understand why he had killed Sandra B. shortly afterwards, who had noticed the exchange of the children, and now Daniel's real father, who wanted to come clean under pressure from the media.

Perhaps, she thought as she switched off the television, it would have been better if the time capsule had never been opened. And perhaps she, Patricia and Marie should never have been involved in this case. Sometimes the truth was too painful to be dragged into the light. But perhaps something new could now be built on the ruins and lies of the past. She opened the window to listen to the birds singing in the evening twilight and sat down to work on her embroidery, which she had neglected for far too long

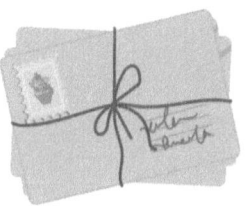

Bon Ami

donalee Moulton

I SHOULD KNOW BETTER than to answer a call from a number I don't recognize. Now, admittedly, as someone who sells novelties (the kind many people like to keep tucked away under the bed), I get a lot of calls from numbers I don't recognize. Any one of them might be wanting to book a Naughty and Nice party complete with scented candles, soft blankets, and passion props—all offered up alongside hors d'oeuvres, petit fours, and sweet tea.

Instead of a booking, I have a woman who keeps telling me her name is Jeanette. I do not know any Jeanettes. She tells me her name again in a raw whisper. "It's Jeanette." I picture her with her hand over the phone, rasping out this information as if somehow I will suddenly sit up, hit my forehead with the palm of my hand, and rasp back, "Eureka! It's Jeanette."

I'm about to hang up when Jeanette repeats her name —and mine. "Ruth, it's Jeanette. Jeanette Comeaux." Nope, nothing. Still don't know any Jeanettes.

After a few seconds' silence, a new voice comes on the line. "Oh, for heaven's sake, Ruth. It's Ashley. Jeanette is my admin assistant."

Turns out, I do know a Jeanette.

CHARLES FONTAINE'S OFFICE IS, in a word, elegant. It befits both his position as Senior Partner at Fontaine LaCroix and his holier-than-thou personality. The back wall is vintage brick; immediately in front is a modern take on a classic bow-legged desk. Cream chairs and sofa are set back from the desk. A black-topped table draws them into a circle. At present, the circle may be unbroken, but it is obviously tense.

Charles is trying to hold court. Ashley, an associate with the firm and the reason I'm here, is hovering. Ashley aced hovering at law school. I do not recognize the man leaning back in the cream armchair, right leg crossed over his left, repeatedly checking his smartwatch. I do not recognize the young man sitting forward in the other armchair, legs crossed at the ankles, repeatedly shooting glances at the man with the watch. I *do* recognize the third person in the room: Odette Marcelin is my client. Was my client. She's a seventeen-year-old high school student with smarts and spunk. Thanks to her quick thinking, another of my clients, her boyfriend, was absolved of felony drug charges earlier this year.

Odette is up and out of her chair. She wraps her arms around me. I squeeze back. Odette nods toward the young man. "You remember the moron."

I do now. This is the boy who planted drugs in her

boyfriend's locker. This would make him Angelo Serafini. And this would make the man with the smartwatch and the air of authority Dominic Serafini. Now I understand why Charles is failing miserably at holding court and why Ashley is hovering. Mr. Serafini runs organized crime in New Orleans. He does this with a steady hand; some would even say a moderate hand. But make no mistake: Serafini Sr. does not hesitate to squash anyone or anything in his way, and nothing will make him lash out more quickly than a threat against his heir apparent.

To his credit, Dominic Serafini lets Odette's snide comment go by the wayside. He stands up and extends his hand. "You must be Ruth Harper. The lawyer."

I want to tell him I am not a lawyer. I sell fantasy toys. It is a mantra that has not taken root. Too many people will point out I'm technically semi-retired and I only sell feathers and infused body mists part time.

I shake Dominic's hand. Odette's look indicates this may be an error in judgment. It's clear everyone knows why we're here but me. Several people rush in to offer explanations.

"We're hoping you can help us resolve an issue." (Charles)

"There's been a development." (Ashley)

"I didn't do nothin'." (Angelo)

"You're still a moron." (Odette)

Got it. I raise my right hand. It takes a few seconds but the cacophony quiets. "I need to speak with my client. In private."

Dominic Serafini steps forward. "I am your client."

The cacophony is back. When silence finally descends, two things are clear. First, Dominic Serafini is not my client.

He does not take this news well. Odette does. She gives me a hug and Angelo the finger.

Dominic shoots Charles a look. It is not a nice look. "You said she'd be my lawyer." Now I shoot Charles a look. Charles looks at Ashley. So, business as usual. We could go round in circles all day. I raise my hand.

"Let's start by telling me why anyone needs a lawyer."

That's when the second thing becomes clear. Odette is being threatened. She received a letter in the mail yesterday —perhaps her first ever from the US postal service. It was brief, and it was nasty.

I'm comin for you

In typical Odette fashion, she did not go to the police, she did not tell her mother, she did not call her lawyer. She went directly to the source. That would be Angelo, he of moron fame. Odette publicly confronted him in school, accused him of sending the letter, and told him, in her words, "Bring it, slick."

Angelo did not bring it. The school principal did—she brought the issue to the attention of both parents. Odette's mom was understandably worried; Odette promised she would call me and we'd go to the cops together. Before she had a chance, Dominic called Fontaine LaCroix and set up this meeting.

And here we are. Exactly nowhere.

Odette thinks further investigation is not necessary. "He did this," she says, pointing to Angelo.

Angelo is on his feet. "Did not." Perhaps not Angelo's most articulate choice of words.

Dominic steps quietly between his son and his son's

accuser. He puts up two hands. The movement is gentle and firm. The room comes to a standstill. He turns to Odette and sighs. "You have made your point. I think you're wrong. Let's find out which one of us is right."

Odette opens her mouth. I fear a repeat of her accusation. She thinks better of it. She looks Dominic in the eye. "I am not afraid of you."

Dominic sighs again. He meets Odette's eyes. There is no animosity here. "Then you are not as bright as I thought you were. You should be afraid of me."

I'm on my feet. "That is a threat. Threats are indictable."

Charles is fluttering around making noises. Ashley is doing the helicopter thing. Odette is standing tall, albeit slightly behind me. Dominic Serafini is smiling.

"People, get a grip. No one is threatening anyone in this room. We are all trying to figure out who threatened the lovely young lady with the foul mouth."

Odette gives him the finger. Really got to give the girl points for having chutzpah, but Dominic Serafini will have a boiling-over point. I don't want to find out what it is.

I switch gears. "Why are you so sure your son did not send this letter?"

Dominic looks around the room. "Do I have any privilege here?"

"You don't. But what you do have," I say to Dominic, "is my word that whatever is said in this room will not be used against you by anyone else in this room." Everyone nods, although I first have to poke Odette in the waist.

That's good enough for Dominic. "For most of my life, I've felt like a dentist. I walk into a room and people want to walk out. Take your fear and magnify it tenfold. Welcome to my son's world."

Angelo hangs his head. His father walks over and puts his arm around his son's shoulders. There is tenderness here. "I love my son. My son loves me. And when I tell my son not to do something, my son does not do it." We all wait for what's to come. I'm not sure anyone in the room is breathing.

Dominic looks at me. He nods. It's an acknowledgement of understanding and respect between two professionals. He looks at Odette and shakes his head. "Ms. Marcelin, my son did not write that letter. I know he did not write that letter because I told him to stay away from you. Very far away."

It's agreed that the threat to Odette may have been made by someone other than Angelo Serafini. Odette wants it on the record that he's still a moron. Dominic Serafini ignores the thorn in his son's side, and his. He has a proposal. He will not become my client, but he will pay my client's bills as we investigate why someone wants to scare Odette, or worse.

"I may want to call in the cops."

"Do what you need to do, Ms. Harper. I want my son cleared of these accusations."

TWO DAYS and ten interviews later, I'm no further ahead. I've spoken with all of Odette's friends, at least everyone who is eighteen and legally no longer a minor. They're all fiercely protective. All except one: Kayla Hill. She's not anti-Odette; she's just not a member of the super-fan club.

According to her, "Odette can be a little extra." I had to look that up when I got home, but the intent was clear from the eye roll and the loud sigh.

Kayla thinks Odette rushed to judgment when she blamed Angelo for writing the letter. Kayla thinks Odette often rushes to judgment "because, of course, she's never wrong."

It's clear Kayla has issues with her friend. That's a far cry from sending a threat through the post. (If bullies knew what they were doing, they'd hand deliver the letter directly to the mailbox themselves and stay clear of the postal service. There are nasty penalties for using the US mail to threaten someone.)

Angelo also has his share of super-fans, and they appear genuine. The four boys I speak to all like Angelo and all firmly believe he didn't send the letter. They know who his father is and what he is (allegedly) capable of. That would seem to rule each of them out as the letter writer.

I was hoping the answer to this would be easy. That hope has been dashed. I'm going to have to go to the next level. Talk to adults.

And I'm going to have to do it quickly. Odette has received a second letter.

Your dead.

THE FIRST ADULT I talk to is Jasper Moore, guidance counsellor at St. Delphine Academy. Once waivers from the two students and their parents land on his highly polished desk, he agrees to talk to me. Jasper has lots to say. No surprise, he is a fan of Odette. Surprise, he is also a fan of Angelo. The former is bright, independent, curious, and driven. The latter is none of those things, but he is something else—and something very important: a survivor.

"I give Angelo full credit for waking up every morning and walking into this school. His father is an albatross; one he loves and one whose weight he will gladly bear for the rest of his life." Jasper says this without emotion or emphasis.

I respond in kind. "He's no angel though, despite his name."

The guidance counsellor gives me a reluctant smile. "I would hazard to guess there is one other thing Angelo isn't. The writer of those letters."

"Because his father told him not to hassle her."

"There is that," Jasper says. "Dominic Serafini is not a man to be trifled with. But planting drugs in a fellow student's locker and getting caught is downright humiliating. I think Angelo has simply had enough. All he wants is to keep his head down and get out of high school as fast as he can."

"Most other kids would be in jail."

"Most other kids don't have Dominic Serafini for a dad."

I ask about Kayla Hill as a possible letter writer. Jasper reminds me he can't talk about any student other than the two for whom he has personal and parental approval.

"Fair enough. Can you answer this question: hypothetically, do you think a student like Kayla Hill would write those letters?"

Jasper doesn't hesitate. "No."

The second adult on my appointment list is the man

himself. Serafini's office takes up the third floor of a high-rise on Poydras Street. I exit the elevator and enter through two glass doors that simply say Serafini Construction. There does not appear to be any security. Appearances can be deceptive; I'm less than three feet into the outer office when a man I didn't see is somehow standing beside me. He holds out his hand. "I'm Dane Mercer, Vice President of Operations. Can I help you?"

Dane Mercer is about 35 and obviously comfortable with his own authority. His shoulders are relaxed, his head tilted, arms casually resting at his side, the left one very near the Glock 19 he is making no attempt to hide and legally does not have to. Louisiana is a constitutional carry state.

"Ruth Harper," I say, shaking his hand. "I'm meeting Dominic." The omission of Serafini's last name is deliberate, and my comfort level with his boss registers with Dane. He tries to hide his surprise at an appointment he wasn't told about. And I'm curious as to why he wasn't.

Dominic Serafini's office is lovely and soft. White oak offset with shades of taupe and hints of teal. I fail to hide my surprise. Dominic looks around the room. "Like it?" There is pride in his voice.

"Very much. I just didn't picture you in an office like this."

"Neither did I. Angelo did this. Kid has always loved design. I told him he could do what he wanted. This is what he wanted."

"He did a very nice job," I say, surprised not at the décor but at the nuances Angelo has hidden. Dominic waves me to a chair. A woman I didn't see anywhere in the outer office glides in with two cappuccinos. A plate of fresh beignets follows. I may visit more often.

We talk about the weather, the Saints, and potholes. Standard fare. Dominic nudges the plate of beignets toward me. I take my second. "I assume you're not here to chat about football."

"I'm here to give you a heads-up—with my client's permission."

Dominic sits back. His shoulders stiffen. He's not going to like what I have to say, but it's not what he thinks it is. "I'd like to tell you something, but I'd like you to keep it confidential for now." I wait until Dominic nods yes. "No one, including my client, believes Angelo sent those letters."

The father in Dominic sighs. His shoulders come closer to earth. He looks at me. The corners of his eyes turn up. "That was the good news. I assume there is bad."

I nod. "It's time to call the cops." I give Dominic a moment to let this settle.

He shrugs. "Do what you have to do."

WHAT I DO IS CALL *the* cop. Singular. I've worked with Bryce Landry, a detective in the Sixth District, on a few cases. He's helpful, practical, open to new ideas. We're looking at one of those ideas now: a crime board in my living room. Bryce and I have decorated it with Post-it notes in a rainbow of colors. We'll sort and sift once we're finished brainstorming. I reach for my glass of Picpoul de Pinet, which sounds a lot more expensive than it is.

Bryce is slouched in an overstuffed armchair, feet resting on a footstool. He reminds me of a mushroom. His forehead is wrinkled, eyes almost closed. "We have no suspects. We're going to need more wine."

This is one of the reasons I like working with Bryce. We order muffuletta pizza to go with the wine. We're trying not to talk about what's on the crime board with the fluffy pink cuffs dangling from one corner (don't ask). All roads lead to nasty letters and a dearth of potential writers.

"Who could hate Odette enough to do this?" Bryce says more to himself than me.

This is my cue to play devil's advocate. "Perhaps we should be asking who loves Angelo enough to come to his defence with guns blazing?"

"Either way the answer is the same," says Bryce. "No one on our crime board."

"So who's not on our crime board?"

Bryce gives me the look all cops are trained to give people who have lost touch with reality. He moves the wine bottle to his side of the table.

I'm sitting up now, index finger pointed upward. "We're assuming this whole letter business is the result of Odette getting her boyfriend off on drug charges—and having them land in Angelo's lap."

"Well, he did plant the drugs," Bryce points out, always the cop.

I wave that bit of reality away. "For now, let's assume the letters have nothing to do with what happened earlier this year."

"That brings us back to our original question. Who hates Odette or Angelo enough to do this?"

Somewhere, just out of reach, is a hypothetical domino. I'm struggling to make it fall into place. "We know Angelo planted drugs in a student's locker. We know Odette fooled Angelo into confessing. We know Angelo doesn't go to jail because he has a scary dad. Everyone goes back to high school like nothing happened."

"Life as we know it," says Bryce.

"Who would want to disrupt that life?"

The answer to that question requires more wine. One bottle and two pints of mango gelato later, we know who is threatening Odette. And we have a dilemma.

THIS TIME DANE MERCER knows I'm coming, and he's waiting for me. His greeting is warm, offhand, like we are old acquaintances. He offers me coffee. I tell him I'll only be a minute. He ushers me into Dominic's office. He doesn't leave. It appears there will be three of us today.

Dominic asks me if there is any reason Dane can't join us. None I can think of. "We won't be long. I was wondering if you and Angelo could come to Fontaine LaCroix tomorrow. I'd like to give everyone an update, and we may have a few questions for Angelo. Routine," I hasten to add.

Dominic isn't buying this. He shrugs off his confusion and looks at me without malice.

"We'll be there." Dominic reaches out his hand.

Dane doesn't have Dominic's restraint. "Everything okay?" he asks as we walk through the outer office.

"Absolutely," I assure him. "Just a few details we need to clarify." I'm almost out the door when a piece of paper sticking out of my jacket falls to the floor. It's the official time sheet from Fontaine LaCroix. Dane is more than happy to help me fill in the blanks. "All I need is for you to put your address, title, and full name here." I hand him a pen and point to the spot on the sheet that logs lawyers' billable hours.

"Didn't think people used these anymore," Dane says, grinning.

I grin back. "We usually don't, but this is an unusual arrangement."

Dane knows exactly what I mean.

WE'RE BACK in Charles Fontaine's office. He's still fluttering, and Ashley is still hovering. Angelo is staring at his Nike Dunks; Odette is staring straight ahead. Dominic is leaning back in his chair, sipping coffee. Odette's mother has joined us. There is a fresh fruit plate, but no one is eating. I thank everyone for coming.

"Did we have a choice?" Angelo asks. He's not being surly. Still, his father shoots him the look parents shoot rude offspring, and Angelo returns to staring at his stylish sneakers.

"We know who is sending the letters to Odette." There is at least one gasp, one white knuckle on the arm of a chair, and a swivel of heads first in my direction, then Odette's. Odette continues to stare straight ahead, but she squeezes her mother's hand.

"Our quandary has been what to do with what we know." I have everyone's attention. I need to take my time. I need everyone in the room to land where Bryce and I, and earlier this morning, Odette, have landed. And by everyone, I mean Dominic Serafini.

"We started from the assumption that this was about Odette. The threatening letters were in response to her run-in with Angelo. Either someone was standing up for Angelo or someone wanted to get even with Odette for tricking Angelo into an admission of guilt. We were wrong."

"What else is there?" This is Angelo. His father, from the look on his face, has asked himself the same question and may be getting closer to the answer.

"This isn't about Odette," I say looking at Angelo. I'm beginning to feel sorry for the kid. "It's about you."

I expected an eruption. Instead, there is dead silence. Angelo is looking from me to his father. Odette gets up and walks towards him. She puts her hand on his shoulder. She sits next to him on the floor and looks up. "I'm so sorry," she says.

Now I am the centre of attention. "Angelo is Dominic's son. Sons carry on from where their fathers leave off. It is assumed Angelo is heir apparent, even if the apparent is sometime in the future. Someone did not want him to have that legacy."

"What are you talking about?" Angelo starts to stand up. Odette squeezes the back of his leg. He sits down. Hard.

"Kid, in your short life, you have messed up. As do we all, although perhaps you have messed up more than most. Someone wants to make it look like you are unworthy of inheriting an empire."

Angelo has no words. He simply shakes his head. He turns to his father. Dominic gets out of his chair and takes his son in his arms. "I'm so sorry," he says. He turns to Odette. "I'm so sorry."

There are only three of us in the room who know what he's sorry for.

As we play out our version of *The Godfather, Part III,*

Bryce Landy is at the offices of Serafini Construction arresting Dane Mercer on state and federal charges. He tried to deny writing the letters, but the letter matched his writing on my timesheet. Dane will be in jail for a long time. The dilemma Bryce and I have had to grapple with is if he will be allowed to live long enough to reach the end of his sentence.

DOMINIC SERAFINI HAS COME to pay his bill in person. He has asked Odette and her mother to join us a little later. I don't know what he wants. I know it is nothing to worry about. Dane Mercer is alive and behind bars.

I have been given a bonus, a very nice bonus. I tell Dominic there is no need. He assures me it is the least he could do. I'm not arguing with the man.

"You were worried I would hurt Dane."

"I was very worried you would hurt Dane. Your second-in-command not only defies you, he jeopardizes your son's future. Honestly, I wanted to hurt him."

Dominic gives me a quick, sad smile. "I will hurt Dane by not hurting Dane."

Despite the poetic ambiguity, I know what Dominic Serafini means. Two things have become quite clear. First, and not surprisingly, Dane Mercer will not cut a deal with NOPD or the feds by undercutting his former boss. He is not that stupid. Second, and perhaps surprisingly, Dominic Serafini is walking away from whatever relationship he had with his vice president of operations. This is a personal response to the situation and a professional one. While there will be no contract put on Dane's life, there will be no protection for him either. That is not a safe place to reside, especially when you reside in jail.

"How is Angelo doing with all this?"

The quick, sad smile is back. "He thought Dane was his friend. It will be good for him to get away. To meet people who do not know who his father is."

Now this is new. "Where is Angelo going?"

"The Rhode Island School of Design." Dominic is beaming as all proud fathers do. "He wants to be an interior designer."

Ashley is at the door with sweet tea, scones, and Odette and her mom. Ashley hovers, but I do not invite her to join us.

"Thank you for coming," Dominic says to Odette. "I wanted to talk to you about something."

Odette also has something to say—to the father of the boy she once called a moron. "Angelo told me about RISD. You must be so happy for him."

"And sad," says Dominic. "You must know that feeling." He looks at Odette's mom. She nods. He turns back to Odette. "My son tells me you have been accepted to Harvard."

"Yes," Odette says with a tenor of pride, "but I have decided to go to LSU."

"Louisiana State is a great school," says Dominic. He looks at me. There is uncertainty in that look, like I know what is going on. He turns to Odette. "If you are interested in attending Harvard, I would be pleased to pay your tuition and expenses for as long as you'd like to attend."

"If I go to Harvard," says Odette, "my goal would be to get into Harvard Law. I want to become a prosecutor. I want to put people like Dane Mercer in prison—and those he works for."

Dominic Serafini understands what Odette is telling him. He does not care. "My offer still stands." He rises from his chair. "I'm sure this is something you'd like to talk about with your mom." He turns to Odette's mother and holds out his hand. "It has been a pleasure to meet you. You've raised a wonderful young woman." When he reaches the door, he turns back to Odette. "Please let me know what you decide."

I realize I'm holding a glass of iced tea like a statue. It's dripping beads of condensation on the desk. I close my mouth and put the glass down.

"Is he serious?" Odette finally says.

"You know as much as I do, but he certainly sounded serious."

"What does he want?"

"I think he wants to say thank you."

"That's quite the apology." Odette rises and comes around my desk. She's only a few feet from me. "I'm worried if I say yes, he'll expect more. I'll owe him. Maybe I'll even want to owe him. Is this the beginning of the slippery slope?"

I reach out and draw her in for a hug. "Odette, your slope will never be that slippery."

The End
Did you enjoy *Signed, Sealed...Deceased*?
Please consider leaving a review on Goodreads, Bookbub, or your favorite retailer.

Join our newsletter for new releases, sales and ucoming events at www.beachesandtrailspublishing.com

Contributors

Lena Samson, Editor 🍁

Lena Samson is an editor and writer living near Ottawa. She serves on the Board of Directors of Ottawa Independent Writers (OIW) and as Editor in Chief of their annual anthology. Lena has edited fiction, alternative history, memoir and children's books (so far), as well as stories in all genres. Retired from the federal public service, Lena enjoys grandmothering, editing, writing and trying to please her fussy pet rabbit.

Andrea Barton

Andrea is the award-winning author of the Jade Riley Mysteries. She runs Brightside Story Studio, a book-editing business, and is Vice President of Mansfield Readers and Writers Festival. She has published short stories, picture books, anthologies, and stage productions. An electrical engineer turned career consultant, Andrea spent twelve years enjoying expat life in Nigeria, the US and Qatar with her husband and two children before repatriating to Australia, where she commutes between Melbourne and Mansfield.

Melissa Behrend

Melissa Behrend is a writer living in the Pacific Northwest with her husband and two dogs, Mayhem and Chaos. She writes short stories, novels, and scripts.

Rachel Desiree Felix

Rachel Desiree Felix is a Malaysian writer based in South Korea. Her work blends Southeast Asian memory with cross-cultural identity to explore language, silence, and survival. She writes fiction and poetry rooted in themes of emotional reclamation, food, and diasporic belonging. When not writing, she enjoys quiet breakfasts, monsoon weather, and returning—through words—to the sea.

Daniel Fox [🇨🇦]

Daniel Fox is a writer of horror, thrillers, fantasy, and children's books. He also created an online choose-your-own-adventure horror video game called *Ocean of Death*. Wow, he should really focus.

Gabbi Grey [🇨🇦]

USA Today Bestselling author Gabbi Grey lives in beautiful British Columbia where her fur baby chin-poo keeps her safe from the nasty neighbourhood squirrels. Working for the government by day, she spends her early mornings writing contemporary, gay, sweet, and dark erotic BDSM romances. While she firmly believes in happy endings, she also believes in making her characters suffer before finding their true love. She also writes m/f romances as Gabbi Black and Gabbi Powell.

Albert Katz [🇨🇦]

After forty-three years working as a cognitive scientist and professor of psychology at Western University, Albert N. Katz retired from academia and started a new career as a writer of short stories and poetry. His poems and stories have appeared in anthologies, genre-based (mystery, horror, science fiction) and literary magazines. His neo-noir crime or mystery stories have appeared (or will appear) in magazines such as *Black Cat Weekly*, *Illustrated Worlds Magazine*, *Mystery Tribune*, and *Punk Noir*.

Daisy Landish [🇨🇦]

Daisy Landish is a sweet romance and cozy mystery author whose clean and heartwarming stories have tugged at readers' heartstrings around the world. Her work has been featured in online magazines and multi-author anthologies, bringing her signature blend of humor, hope, and happily-ever-afters to an ever-growing readership. When she's not crafting love stories, Daisy spends her time reading, hiking at dawn, and riding into the sunset on her horse, Rosebud.

Denise Landry 🇨🇦

Denise Landry is a disabled writer living in Montreal, Canada. Her poems and short stories have been published in several magazines and small press anthologies. Publishers include Sweetycat Press/Steve Carr (2022), Written Tales Chapbooks (2023, 2024), Wicked Shadow Press (2023), Pen and Paw International (2024), River City Siren Press (2024), and *Micromance* magazine (2024).

Iris March

Iris March has a reputation for killing house plants and now she's killing people off in books. Coincidence? Perhaps not. Iris has spent two decades working in the sustainability field and is usually either reading a book or on a trail. She lives in Ohio with her husband, son, and three cats. Learn more about upcoming books and sign up for her newsletter on her website.

Flora McGowan

Flora McGowan is the author of the *Carrie and Keith Mysteries*, novels and short stories, including a contribution to the charity anthology *The Little Shop of Murders*. Her stories combine a mix of mystery with the mystical and supernatural, an historical element as well as a touch of humour and a dash of romance. Flora was born in Dorset and many of her stories are based in this area.

donalee Moulton 🇨🇦

donalee Moulton's first mystery, *Hung out to Die*, was published in 2023. *Conflagration!* won the 2024 Daphne du Maurier Award for Excellence in Mystery/Suspense (Historical Fiction). donalee has two books out in 2025: *Bind* and *Melt*, the first two mysteries in the Lotus Detective Agency series. 'Swan Song,' published in *Cold Canadian Crime*, was shortlisted for an Award of Excellence and 'Troubled Water' was shortlisted for a 2024 Derringer Award and a 2024 Award of Excellence.

Andrea Tillmanns

Andrea Tillmanns lives in Germany and works full-time as a university lecturer. She has been writing poetry, short stories and novels in various genres for many years. Her poems and stories have been published in numerous magazines and anthologies. More information about the author and her texts can be found on her website.

BEACHES AND TRAILS PUBLISHING

About the Publisher

Beaches and Trails Publishing is an independent Canadian press based in Quebec, dedicated to uplifting stories that comfort, inspire, and empower. We believe in the power of inclusive, positive, and accessible fiction.

Our catalogue highlights a diversity of Canadian voices—especially emerging authors and writers from underrepresented communities

At Beaches and Trails, every book is an invitation to feel good—and to feel seen.

www.beachesandtrailspublishing.com

instagram.com/beachesandtrailspublishing
facebook.com/beachesandtrailspublishing
amazon.com/author/beachesandtrailspublishing
linkedin.com/company/beaches-and-trails-publishing
pinterest.com/beachesandtrailspublishing
x.com/BAT_publishing

www.ingramcontent.com/pod-product-compliance
Lightning Source LLC
Chambersburg PA
CBHW030305060726
47498CB00002BB/511